PROMISE KEPT

PROMISE KEPT

STEPHANIE PERRY MOORE

KENSINGTON PUBLISHING CORP.
http://www.kensingtonbooks.com

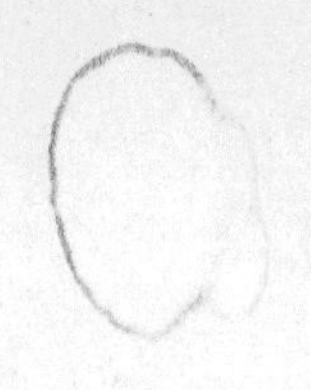

DAFINA BOOKS are published by

Kensington Publishing Corp.
850 Third Avenue
New York, NY 10022

All Kensington titles, imprints and distributed lines are available at special quantity discounts for bulk purchases for sales promotion, premiums, fund-raising, educational or institutional use.

Special book excerpts or customized printings can also be created to fit specific needs. For details, write or phone the office of the Kensington Special Sales Manager: Kensington Publishing Corp., 850 Third Avenue, New York, NY 10022. Attn. Special Sales Department. Phone: 1-800-221-2647.

ISBN-13: 978-0-7582-2540-5
ISBN-10: 0-7582-2540-7

First Kensington Trade Paperback Printing: May 2008
10 9 8 7 6 5 4 3 2 1

Printed in the United States of America

For Nicole (my dear friend).
Best friends are supposed to keep their promise!
Unfortunately, not all do.
Take comfort in knowing, my strong friend,
that God is with you.
As we go through, may we all remember
that He always keeps His word.

Acknowledgments

Doesn't it just tick you off when folks don't keep their word? Some mess you up so much when they back out of their commitment that you don't want to fool with them anymore. Guess God has a right to be angry with us when we back out of what we commit to Him, huh? Well thankfully, He gives us grace. Unfortunately, the judicial system isn't so kind. You break the law, you pay.

I was watching the news the other night and saw a case where someone was accused of something he didn't do and needed a good legal team to get him off. I got to thinking, in writing a book I always need a good writing team to help me get out a good novel. Now that I'm at the end of the series I feel like I'm on trial. I promised to be committed to a series that would move young people to walk right for Him. Did I stay true to my cause? Well, I think so. And here is a thank you for all the folks that held me accountable to doing just what I said I would.

To my family, parents Dr. Franklin and Shirley Perry Sr., brother Dennis and sister-in-law Leslie, my mother-in-law Ms. Ann, and extended family Bobby and Sarah Lundy, and

Walter and Marjorie Kimbrough, and Paul and Tammy Garnes, you remind me of a great defense team. You always back me up. Like a tenacious defense law firm, thanks for keeping me out of trouble.

To my publisher, Kensington/Dafina Books, and the distribution companies that move the product, especially Pam Nelson at Levy Books. I appreciate you constantly helping me get my books out there. My message is heard with you on the team. Like the truthful broadcaster ready to tell the world the events that unfold, you help me make sure the world knows they need to get behind what I've got to share.

For my writing team, Calvin Johnson, James Johnson, Ciara Roundtree, Jessica Phillips, Randy Roberts, Ron Whitehurst, Vanessa Davis Griggs, Larry Spurill, John Rainey, Carolyn O'Hara, Jason Spellen, Teri Anton, and the Georgia Tech Parent Buzz organization, you hold me accountable to every word. Thanks for combing over the pages to make sure it will hit home to many. Like an accurate court reporter, you help me tell it like it is.

To the dynamic and talented authors that were with me on the historic first African-American Levy Bus tour: my Dafina cohorts Daaimah Poole, Earl Sewell, Rochelle Alers, Brenda Jackson, Francis Ray, Lori Bryant Woolridge, Teri Woods, Donna Hill, Nina Foxx, Selena Montgomery, Grace Akallo, Francis Ray, Naleighna Kai, ReShonda Tate Billingsley, Nikki Turner, Crystal Hubbard, Trisha R. Thomas, Tracie Howard, and my dear author mentor Beverly Jenkins, you are my witnesses that writing isn't in vain. Thanks for your support and I pray your books keep blessing many. Like a good witness, we can attest to the impact our books have on the world.

To my girlfriends Jackie Dixon, Jenell Clark, Loni Perriman, Gloria London, Taiwanna Bolds, Tabatha Palmer, Deborah Bradley, Cynthia Peace, Vickie Davis, Kim Monroe, Jan Hatchett, Veida Evans, Joy Nixon, Lakeba Williams, and Perlicia Floyd, you are the best parents I know. I know God placed you in my life for such a time as this. Like a sound therapist, you confirm to me that though I live mostly in a made-up world and write about much drama, I'm sane.

To my children, Dustyn Leon, Sydni Derek, and Sheldyn Ashley, I wish I could give you the world. Though I can't, I can give you the key that holds everything you'll need . . . Love and serve God and you'll be more than fine. Like the posse that surrounds most defendants, you keep me going when the going gets rough.

To my beau, Derrick Moore, I'm stronger with you by my side. Though you are swamped, please keep your word and read more of my stuff. Like a prison guard that any defendant tries to befriend for lenience, you are strong, never waver, don't bend the rules, but protect me well.

To my readers, I'm hoping you all get on my writing bandwagon to stay. I pray each book in the Perry Skky Jr. series stirred your soul to live for Him. Like a unified jury, always stand for justice and lock the enemy away.

And to my precious Savior, You helped me complete another series. I pray I have pleased You with each book. You are the only judge that matters.

Contents

1. Trying to Win 1

2. Dealing with Trouble 15

3. Clinging to Hope 25

4. Recruiting New Ideas 37

5. Showing True Feelings 49

6. Following the Soul 59

7. Checking Things Out 69

8. Getting into Danger 81

9. Calming My Heart 93

10. Running from Love 103

11. Circling the Wagons 113

12. Spreading God's Word 123

13. Pouting for Sure 133

14. Feeling Real Joy 143

15. Finding Our Way 153

~ 1 ~

Trying to Win

Okay, I couldn't believe that Savoy just slapped me. It was Christmas break and everyone was hanging out at Howard's Bar-be-que, in my home town. I was with my boys, Cole and Damarius and some chicks were hanging around us, but I was being a good boy. I only had a few days till I had to head back to school and get ready to play in the National Championship college game.

After the slap, I didn't know how to feel. First of all, it hurt. So I was pissed. Second, my boys were just sitting there looking at me like they knew I wasn't going to take it. So I was angry.

Then I looked into Savoy's eyes. Through the tears that began to fall from her lashes, I could see she was hurting. So I felt bad. There was a little crowd of honeys watching and though I didn't want to be punked, something was going on with my girl.

"You two, don't even say anything to me!" I shouted to Damarius and Cole.

Damarius jerked me by the back of my shirt and said, "I know you ain't gon' just let her talk to you like that."

"It's obvious that something is wrong with her. Can't you see? Come on, man. Give me some space," I said as I pulled away from Damarius.

"Aight, aight! Whatever, but you the one that's gonna miss out on all the fun," he said as he tapped Cole and they walked a few feet away.

Savoy just looked at me and wiped her face. I knew she was disappointed and for whatever reason she thought I had let her down. I could understand her being upset and all, but to come at me swinging and hitting me in public was unacceptable.

Her first semester in college must have been harder than I thought for her to lash out at me this way. Her bold gesture was dumb. We were working on rebuilding what we had after deciding to get back together. Just because I didn't play things her way she was going to pitch a fit, like some out-of-control toddler. I took a deep breath and motioned her to talk to me. After all, since she'd made such a bold stand to call me out, she certainly had something to say.

Savoy angrily snarled, "I can't believe you! You haven't talked to me in two days. And before that, you claimed you were *so* busy. Either you got to work out or you got to hang out with the guys. You've got to do something for your mom or dad. Shucks, you don't even have time for me. Then my brother gets me out of the house and I find you flirting with a whole bunch of high school girls. You better be careful, or else you'll be in jail for child molest . . ."

"Okay, see, I've had enough," I told her quickly, cutting her off. "Why are you being the over-jealous type?"

When she looked down, unable to respond, I figured maybe every girl had it in her. I could relate. I was certain that I didn't want to see her with another guy, but she shouldn't just assume that I was dissing her. I knew that no matter what I said, there was no way I was going to win. "So you can't answer me? You can't respond."

She shook her head. "Naw, I know you won't understand."

I said, "Try me. Say *something*. I don't appreciate you trying to humiliate me."

"You care more about what everybody else thinks instead of what I think."

"No, you don't respect me."

"Like you respect me," she said. "Please, Perry, if you did you wouldn't lie to me. We'd be together. You'd make me a priority."

She just went on and on whining. It was so annoying. I had a lot of pressure on me. A lot of people were pulling on me from all different kinds of directions. We said we were going to be an item, wasn't that enough for her?

"Just forget it, Perry. I don't even know why I try. I don't even know why I cared."

She left the restaurant. Like a nut, I followed her. I thought about my sister Payton. If there was one thing I had learned from her, it was that during a certain time of the month girls went cuckoo. Maybe that was the case with Savoy, so I went over.

Gently, I stroked her soft brown hair. "So is it that time of the month for you or something?"

"Why does it have to be all of that? Can it be that I just want you to care? I don't understand why it's so hard for you to understand."

"You can't put limitations on me."

"I didn't."

"I'd think you'd understand that I haven't seen my friends or my family in practically months. With all that I have had to balance—from trying to be an A student to showing out on the field—it's just been one thing after another. Finally, I get the good news that I'm going to have the chance to play in the big game and I can't even celebrate." I sighed. "I mean, if you want to know everywhere I go, if you want to sign off on every little thing I do, then honestly this might be too much for me."

"Okay, forgetting me, putting me aside, Perry, could you honestly say that the Lord would be pleased at what you're doing right now? Don't you think that He would see your actions as a little suspect for a guy who is supposed to have a girlfriend?"

"Savoy, the Lord knows what's in my heart and I know He wouldn't condemn me because of something Damarius does. Yeah, he has five girls hanging on him, but they ain't hanging on me."

"Whatever. They are not around him because of him. Everybody knows who you are. I have heard the buzz. Every girl in this barbeque joint wants you smothered between two slices of toasted bread. You've got 'potential millionaire' written all across your forehead. Are you stupid? Do you not see?" Savoy came at me worse than an attack dog.

Standing my ground, I said, "I told you I didn't want a jealous girlfriend." It was almost like she was about to hyperventilate, so I paused.

"Well, excuse me, but if you would be more of a boyfriend, and give me the same things that you expect from me, we wouldn't have these issues. And to answer your question from earlier, yes, I'm on my period right now. So I'm sorry for hitting you in public and all that. I wasn't trying to embarrass you. I was trying to get your attention; either you want to be in this relationship with me or you don't."

"Well, it can't be just your way. If you're saying those are the terms, then bye."

She turned around and threw her hands up in the air. Deep down I cared a lot about her. Way more than I ever did for Tori. I loved her, I just wanted to be cautious and keep my heart guarded. I wasn't trying to downplay all that she was saying, but I didn't see myself as all that either. Maybe God could help me to check myself.

Alright, Lord, if I'm wrong for having a little time for me, show me. If I'm supposed to be with Savoy, You need to show me how she and I can make it.

Damarius and Cole walked up to me and Damarius said, "That's what I'm talking about. Let her walk away. You the man!"

When I was back at Georgia Tech in Atlanta, Coach Red addressed the team in a frustrated tone. "Men, I'm disappointed in you. You've got to be self-motivated to make it to the top. No one can give you the desire to become the best. You've got a National Championship game to play and I know most of you went home for the full week off I gave you. Now most of you look like you haven't even worked out while away from our trainers and the facility."

The talk was that coach had been going crazy. We knew it was stress from sportswriters speculating that another team should have gotten in the big game, not us. We heard we got voted in because of the politics Coach played. He had a lot of pressure on him.

I didn't know why he thought we were unfocused, why he thought we didn't care. Just because we wanted to be around our families didn't mean that we weren't taking this seriously. I scanned the room and knew every player in there had the heart to win. Saxon raised his hand.

"Yes, Lee. What do you want?" Coach Red snapped.

"Coach, I just wanted to say that you told us we could go home. If that's not what you wanted, why'd you say it was alright?"

"I wanted you guys to make the decision to stay. When you're about to play in a big game, the biggest one you'll ever play in your life, you forgo some things. This National Championship game is *it*; you're getting a chance to play at the most outstanding level. I wanted my men to think, to be in the Championship game and to perform that night while millions are watching. You got to be on your toes. You got to be willing to sacrifice. If you say you want to win, you've got to give it your all," he said, shaking his head. "Yeah, I told you

you could go, but I didn't think you would. But I can't cry over spilt milk. Y'all are going to clean it up. Get out there and do a hundred suicides up and down the stadium steps."

We all grumbled.

"GET OUT THERE NOW!" he yelled.

Quickly, we fled out to the stadium. A line formed and we jogged the stairs. Of course, after twenty-five we were all tired.

"This proves my point. You guys didn't train hard enough this week. But that's okay because we're going to be ready for USC. Those Trojans are going to be ready for a war and we're going to give them one. Strap on your swords, bees, and let's lead 'em on to the hive," he said as our team got fired up.

Two days later, we were on a plane heading down to Miami. I had always heard that the bowl games were something special, but to be in the biggest bowl was something special all in itself. And to play in it as a freshman, I truly was psyched.

As soon as we got there, the hotel's upscale lobby was swarming with press like we were celebrities or something.

Lenard came up to me with one of the other defensive guys and said, "Alright, bonding time."

"Just because we have the night off doesn't mean we need to go out on the town," I said, reminding them of the coach's philosophy. Just because an opportunity presents itself doesn't mean you have to seize it.

Lenard grabbed me by my collar and said, "Quit being a wimp. You're supposed to enjoy this time. You may have an opportunity to come back out here, but as seniors this is our last shot. We are up in the house and Miami here we come. You coming with us?"

"Yeah, I'm coming to keep y'all out of trouble," I said reluctantly. He was right—we wouldn't be here together like this again.

* * *

Unfortunately, the spot we chose was a bar full of Trojan fans. It wouldn't have been that big a deal, but Lenard was sporting his Jackets jersey. The crazy looks we got were eerie.

As soon as we ordered from the bar, a drunk bald guy yelled out, "The sorry Yellow Jackets are in the house."

I said, "Let's just go, guys."

"Nah-unh. I'm not about to leave without my drink," Lenard said.

I didn't have a good feeling, but what could I do? We sat down at a table, and tried to mind our own business and wait for the waitress to come and take our food orders. Then the same drunk fool came up to us with a few of his buddies and started a brawl.

He said, "I know you guys don't think you're going to win."

"Alright, man. Whatever. Nobody is mad that you're a Trojans fan. Just get out of our face and we're cool." Lenard said, and held up his hand in a peace sign.

Unfortunately, the guy didn't go away. "I know your new little freshman quarterback thinks he did good in the ACC Championship game, but we're gonna smash his head in. Who does he think he is? He's so stupid that he got himself ejected for betting on the games. Well, you better get ready to lose because your tired defense ain't much better. Shucks, you all shouldn't have even been playing in this game."

"Okay, I've had enough of him, y'all." Markus stood up and pushed the guy into a corner.

It was on then, with everyone fighting from one end of the bar to the other. At first I watched, but if I was anything, I was loyal. There were only a few of us, so my punches had to count. In no time, I heard sirens and folks started scattering.

I grabbed Lenard off of a man, then yanked on Markus. I shouted, "We've got to get out of here *now!*"

But before we could get away, the police herded us into a corner with the rest of the customers. I couldn't believe the mess we were in. It didn't take law enforcement long to figure out who we were and haul us away. It seemed like an even shorter time passed before an angry Coach Red showed up at the precinct.

"Lenard! Perry! What is up with this? You've already been suspended for fighting."

Lenard rushed to answer. "Folks started coming at us with bottles and stuff. What are we supposed to do?"

Coach snarled, "You shouldn't have been out there in the first place."

At the same time I was thinking, *Yeah, that's what I told them.* But at that moment, what could I have done? I wasn't strong enough to lead them to do the right thing. So I gave in to the pressure and let them lead me into doing something that was wrong. We had cuts on our faces, and Lenard was holding his ribs. We had a National Championship game to play and some of the key players were banged up over this foolishness.

Coach lectured us all the way back to the hotel. I heard him, but he couldn't have made me feel more like a loser.

"It ain't like he's gonna bench us," Markus said as he leaned over and clutched his stomach.

"You know what?" Coach said. "I heard that. All three of you guys are going to sit out the first quarter of this game."

"You want to make that stupid move, Coach, then do what you got to do," Lenard yelled back. What was he thinking?

Coach replied, "Since you're so big and bad, when you get a chance to play, make up the difference. Fight on the field!"

Lenard lowered his voice a few decibels and said, "But you're tying our hands, Coach, by keeping us out one quarter."

Coach Red said, "What's fair is fair. Yes, I want to win a National Championship, but more than that, I want to make you guys winners in life. Actions come with consequences." Now you'll never forget how much your stupid actions cost your team and your fans.

Back at the hotel, Saxon said, "Coach can kiss off." Word of our punishment had got through to the team.

My roommate and our new quarterback, Lance Shadrach, chimed in, "Yeah, if you're not playing, I'm not playing either."

Since Mario, our former starting quarterback, got caught up in a scandal, Lance was ready for the job. He showed out at the Atlantic Coast Conference Championship Game and we won. Though the media was saying we wouldn't have a chance against the Trojans, Lance had the heart of a warrior. I called him a brother in white skin and I knew he was going to show up and do his part on game night. But he and Saxon were talking foolishness. Before I could set them straight, Deuce, our other roommate and running back for the team, echoed Lance's sentiments.

"If the quarterback and tailback don't play, or at least threaten not to, Coach Red will change his dumb tactics. What's he going to do without all of us?"

The three of them went on and on about how they were going to convince the other players to boycott. I was just so thankful that I didn't get arrested like the rest of the club members, for inciting a riot at the Miami bar, that sitting out one quarter of the football game was really no big deal. Even though it was the biggest football game played in college sports.

Deuce came over to me and rested his hand on my shoulder and said, "Look, if it wasn't for you taking time out to help me study, I wouldn't get through school. Seriously, if you hadn't stepped up and made me get all of that calculus, I'd be sitting out the whole game. I know Lenard and Markus, man. They convinced you to go somewhere you didn't want to go. All that football hazing is a bunch of crap. For real you shouldn't be punished for what coach practically signed off on. He told us to follow the upper classmen when the season first started. I'm going to talk to the rest of the team now."

As Deuce headed to the door I just shook my head. I couldn't believe the chump was serious. Why would he put his career on the line for me? Yeah, we were brothers now in every true sense of the heart, and as crazy as Saxon had been towards me—not wanting me to be with his sister and feeling he was a much better player than I was—somewhere along the way he and I had formed a bond too. I cared about those three guys and I needed to let them know that there was no way I was going to let them carry through with any sort of plan of rebellion. I jogged over to the door and barricaded myself in front of it.

"Move, Perry, now move," Deuce said, as he tried unsuccessfully to push me aside.

"Naw, now for real you guys are going to hear me out," I said boldly to the three of them. "Quit being hotheads for a second and listen to me. Saxon, I've been watching you in practice lately and boy, you are a heck of a football player. You know I never wanted to admit that with me and you being rivals in high school and all, but you the man! With me on the bench you're going to get a chance to play. You can show out and show 'em the threat and presence of what's coming next year. Aight?"

"I hear you, man," Saxon said, and he came and gave me dap.

"And Deuce and Lance, though the loyalty chokes me up inside," I said facetiously.

Lance grabbed a pillow and tossed it my way. I ducked. We all laughed.

I continued, "I'm serious. I appreciate y'all caring, but what good is it going to do with none of us in the game? Somebody has to represent the freshman class and help us win this thing. I'ma get back in there. What I want y'all to get is that we got to live by rules, and when you break them you got to step up, be a man, and take what's coming to you. I don't need y'all to take my medicine for me. I know what I did and I know why I did it. I just need the three of y'all out there. And light up the scoreboard, so when I get in I won't have to show y'all up."

They charged me. The next thing you know the four of us were play wrestling. It was cool to know I wanted the best for them and that they had my back.

The next couple of days were chaos. All the sportswriters were clamoring outside the hotel to make the story even bigger than it was. Coach protected Lenard, Markus, and myself through a lot of the public functions that the team went to—team meet-and-greets, pep rallies, Fellowship of Christian Athletes breakfast—so we were able to chill.

I was also avoiding my folks. I knew they had driven down to Miami. I was successful in not seeing them until my dad banged on the hotel room door and yelled that Coach told him I was in there.

"Alright Dad, but I got a game in the morning," I said, sounding real tired.

"Whatever, son, open the door. I need to talk to you now."

I couldn't even look his way. Feeling bad was an understatement. I hated letting my parents down. What could I say?

"I know, Dad. I made a bad decision."

"I hear you, son, but you can't just run away from us when you get in some trouble. Besides, this year you have had one incident after another and we have always been there for you."

"I shouldn't have embarrassed you guys, Dad. Truthfully, you couldn't be more bummed out with me than I am with myself."

He went on anyway, lecturing me for another thirty minutes, then told me to rest up for the game. I appreciated that at the end of the day he brought our conversation back to a positive place.

As he prepared to leave, he touched my shoulder and said, "Listen. All this talk now is that you're coming off of the bench and you won't be able to help the game. Shut the media and the fans up; do your thing tomorrow, aight?"

"Aight, I'ma try," I laughed, trippin' that my pops was down.

Eyeing me to make sure I took him seriously, he said, "Naw, you gon' do it. You hurting this team on the bench. You get in that game and make up the difference."

He had no idea how right he was. In the first quarter we were down 28-0. Saxon was dropping passes. Deuce was getting blocked turn after turn, and Lance was getting sacked every snap. It was a massacre!

In the second quarter Lenard and I were able to join the game. We gave Lance confidence and the O line started blocking better. Deuce was able to run and he scored a touchdown. With Markus back as a leader on defense, we held them, and I caught some crazy balls and scored two touchdowns.

Even with all that battling, when the end of the fourth quarter came we were still behind 28-21. Though we did our best, USC did not come up short. I wanted to beat the Trojans so bad. After all, we lost the first game of the season to them. I played a big part in that loss. My absence in the first quarter of this game will always be in the back of my mind.

Once again, I let my teammates down. As we walked to the middle of the field to shake hands with the victorious Trojans, Coach Red didn't even look my way. I know he was pissed at me. Though we played a hard-fought game, in the end it just wasn't enough simply trying to win!

~ 2 ~

Dealing with Trouble

The mood in the locker room was somber at best; some young men were crying, and rightfully so. For the seniors they'd never get another chance for that ring.

Coach Red said, "Men, we only lost two games all year, we have to take our hats off to the Trojans. I know you're mad at me about the decisions that I made and maybe you're equally upset at some of your teammates for not thinking on this bowl trip. But guys, we have to put this behind us. We had a heck of a season. Nobody gave us anything. We were always ranked in the ugliest spots. Most games we were favored to lose. You guys are champions in my book. Every single one of you is a winner. You may cause me a lot of pain, but one thing for sure, we came together as a team. You need to know wherever you go in life you're someone special."

A few guys cheered, even more clapped. His speech was moving, but it didn't move me. I said to myself I was never going to be depressed again. I wanted to keep my self-esteem intact. However, even with two of the longest catches of my football career, a 97-yarder and a 98-yarder, maybe if I had been in the game sooner I could have done more. I sat down on the bench, placed my head between my knees and let the tears mix in with my sweat.

Then I heard Calvin's voice yell out, "OFFENSE, man, y'all were terrible out there. Y'all didn't block nobody!" I looked up and he was in the face of two of our linemen.

"You need to get out of my face," our center said to him. "That's the problem with you now, Calvin, you can't keep your emotions in check; starting some fight at the bar, getting some of our players suspended because they're trying to support your stupid ways."

"Oh, you calling me stupid?" Calvin said to him as he pushed him into another guy.

Bilboa jumped into the scene and pushed Calvin into another corner. "Naw, he's trying to blame me for him playing poorly." I heard more arguing but I put my head back down.

"You can't blame yourself for this," Deuce came over and said to me.

"Nice try, buddy, but that one don't fly."

"I'm serious man; I choked up in the beginning. You told me it was going to be my time to shine and all I had to do was hold it down until you got in the game, and I choked. You saw more in me than I saw in myself and then when you did come in you put us in a position to almost win it. My yards were the worst of all this year—twenty-two. Now come on, I know your folks want to say something to you. Let's shower and then go enjoy the night. We don't have to fly back until tomorrow."

"I know you didn't just say *enjoy* the night."

"Perry, what you gon' do, wallow in it, man? Learning some lessons? No mistake about it, we got to the big dance because we were good. We're just freshmen and nobody going to think we can get back here next year. But we can, if we take tonight, shake it off, and get ready for this time next year."

"Alright man, I hear you," I agreed, so he would leave me the heck alone. When I went out into our crowd, my parents had a look of pity in their eyes. It took my mom all she had inside of her to say something positive, which wasn't her style because she used to shoot straight at me.

She said to me, "Son, you did so good."

"Yeah, son, you really did," my dad agreed. Man, both of them were crazy. How could I have done such a great job if I was out of the game because of foolishness? I just wasn't trying to be around them or anybody else. People were saying stuff to me, asking me for my autograph as I meandered my way through the crowd, not stopping until Savoy stepped in front of me. The way we left things a week ago, I didn't know where we stood. With everything going on, she actually hadn't been on my mind.

I appreciated it when she said, "I know you got to be hurting, I'm sorry it went down like that. Let's just go out tonight, take your mind off of some of it." She kissed me on the cheek, nibbled on my ear a bit, and I sort of pushed her away.

"Naw, I'm just going to go back to the hotel." I knew she and her parents had come all this way to support the team, but I just couldn't handle any company right now.

"Me and some of the other track girls are going out. I thought you would have missed me this week, but you're still going and putting everything in your life first. Cool, fine. Go back to the hotel and relax then."

I did not feel like putting up with her crap. I had just lost a National Championship game. How dare she try to brush it under the rug. Did she think that her little peck was going to make me forget what had just slipped away?

"Hey, I didn't think we were together no way, from what you said last week," I retorted in anger.

"Oh, dumb me. You're right!" She turned around, flung her hair in my face and walked away. I tried to grab her but more fans stepped between us. I towered over most of them and could see that as she walked away she wasn't even looking back. I'm done with it; maybe she was right. Maybe it shouldn't have been all about me. But if Deuce couldn't understand it, my parents couldn't understand it, and Savoy couldn't understand it—then maybe God would just let me wallow.

On the bus to the hotel I sat in my seat and prayed, *Lord, this is a lot to deal with. Help me to not get into a funk, although I am already in one. Help me to not stay that way! I don't know what I'm saying, Lord, I'm just a frustrated man and really upset. I'm upset at me. The more and more I try to do the right thing, the more negative comes my way. I know You're up there—could you light up my path a little bit? I'm a football player playing in the dark—give me some lights, Lord. Shine some, Lord, dang.*

It was such an emotional, draining day I couldn't wait for my head to hit the pillow and crash. The National Championship game had slipped through my fingers and I wanted that day to be over. However, I heard a bunch of noise at the door when Deuce came in with Saxon and a few other players. I was frustrated that I had not locked the door when they burst in.

"Get up, get up, get up!" Saxon said, messing with my legs.

"Ouch, boy, I'm sore," I told him.

"Aw Perry, come on, man, we're just trying to have a little fun. Get up out the bed, it's not even eleven-thirty. You crashing early like you some little momma's boy or something."

"Sax, you know me well enough to know that little snide comments like that do not bother me. I'm tired, man," I said, putting the pillow over my head. That was stupid because the next thing I knew Deuce and Saxon were pushing me and hitting me and shoving me.

"Alright, alright," I said as I sat up. "What do y'all want?"

Deuce said, "Come on, we are going to hang out for a little bit. We're going to this little club that the track girls are going to."

"Forget them, I hear some of the local girls are fine too—I hear the place is jumping. Let's go," Saxon said.

"Y'all go mess with the honeys," I told them.

"Well, you know my sister is going to be mad that you're not there," Saxon said as he gave me some evil eye, like I wasn't taking care of my business.

"I don't think me and Savoy are going to work out," I said, regretting that I gave her brother more information than he needed.

"Boy, I can tell in your face that you want my sister. And no matter how much I try and fight it—your little having-no-sex behind is the perfect one I want for her. What y'all done had, one time in two years?" I gritted my teeth at his insinuation that I was less of a guy or something because I wasn't trying to screw her brains out. I had integrity and character and I respected her. And more than that, I wanted to respect the word of the Lord, who said that satisfying my flesh had given me too many issues. The last thing I wanted to do was to hurt Savoy's feelings. Maybe I would surprise her and go to the little club, get our groove on and let her take my mind off the game.

So when I got out of the bed Saxon said, "Now, that's what I'm talking about, boy. Yeah, let's go."

Half an hour later we pulled into a club called Heat. None of us were over twenty-one, but flashing our Georgia Tech badges we were able to get in. I checked out my environment—folks were in groups laughing and enjoying each other. There wasn't too much alcohol out, just a few cans and some cigarettes, and people on the dance floor were getting their groove on.

I did not see Savoy, but Deuce said to me, "Oh, there are our girls."

I looked in the direction he was pointing and then our jaws dropped when we saw the Tech girls hanging out with some older local guys.

"I don't understand what's up with this, Kendall knew I was coming. That dude needs to take his hands off her butt. You coming?"

"Naw, man, Savoy looks like she having a good time. She don't need me. I'ma chill over here."

Deuce walked a couple of steps farther and waved his hand at Kendall. She looked up and saw him and met him halfway. I watched as his tongue slid down her throat. I don't know if he was trying to prove a point to the guys that she had just walked away from, that she was his, or if he really was excited about seeing her. Either way, they were cool and went off into a corner somewhere. Savoy, though, tried to play me. She saw me and I smiled. She didn't smile back, just turned around and started rubbing on some guy's chest. It had to be to make me angry, because he wasn't hot. The guy looked like a thug, with one gold tooth in his mouth and a bandana around his head. Yet when I saw him pull out a roll and hand it to his boy for drinks, I realized that he was probably the leader of the crew that she was with. Did she even know what she was doing? It could be dangerous for her to act like she wanted to be with this guy. Accepting a drink from him could get her into even more trouble. The dude could spike her drink or he could take that as a sign that she was his for the rest of the evening. I had to be real and understand what I had done to push her toward this situation in the first place. She was a big girl. She wasn't a baby. But I did sort of hurt her feelings—twice—telling her that I wanted to do something without her. But there was no denying that I cared for her deeply. I felt my blood boiling as I saw the guy run his hand up the back of her shirt.

Saxon came off the dance floor and said to me, "Man, what's up with my sister?"

I couldn't even speak, I just pointed over at her. He saw what I saw. It looked like she was getting herself into a situation that was more than she could handle.

"Man, I think them dudes are in a gang. Now my sister trying to put on a show for you. Y'all so dumb. Y'all like each other. Now she's with this guy in a gang."

"You sure he's in a gang?" I asked. Saxon and I stood up when we saw the guy yank her hand and pull her close to him.

"Ouch!" she screamed out, "let me go. Let me go!" He raised his hand and smacked her. I was about to head on over there when Saxon pushed me down.

"Man, please, I got this."

I said I'd go off to find Deuce so we would be there for back-up if need be. I was so mad at Savoy and mad at myself too. She and I didn't know how to communicate with each other. We had to handle this mess.

"It's a fight, man, it's a fight!" some dude said, running in the direction of the commotion Saxon created. A swarm of people ran past in an effort to see a brawl. I couldn't believe I was the only one with sense, going away from all the fuss. Unfortunately I needed to find Deuce and take my tail back into the midst of the chaos to bail Saxon out. Problem was, I couldn't find Deuce and Kendall anywhere. The noise behind me grew louder and people were yelling, clapping, and cheering. Somebody was getting clobbered, and because my guy wasn't a hometown boy I had a strange feeling Sax was really in trouble.

I jetted up the stairs to the V.I.P. lounge and it was completely empty. I couldn't imagine Deuce talking his way into the V.I.P. section, but I had to check. Even the bouncer that manned the section was downstairs watching the fight. My boy was in trouble. When I saw blood, I reached into my pocket and got my cell out and immediately called 9-1-1. I had been part of the scene only days before, and I knew how this town worked. Whoever they caught would be looking at a rap sheet, whoever called it in would be considered a crime fighter.

"Thanks for your call," the policeman told me, "but the bar owner already called it in and we've got officers headed to the scene. If it's the gang you're describing, I'd recommend you stay clear of them. They're usually armed and more than dangerous."

My breathing intensified tenfold when I hung up the phone. I tried to dial Deuce's phone number three times, in such a state of panic that I misdialed. Finally I got through, only to receive his voicemail. After looking everywhere, I thought about the one place I hadn't looked—the women's bathroom. As soon as the door creaked I heard sounds of passion. Kendall and Deuce were in there making out, trying to get laid up, whatever he wanted to call it. Now just wasn't the time for all that.

"Deuce?"

"Man, what? Not now."

"Saxon's in a fight."

Deuce busted out of the handicap stall with his pants down. I turned around and said, "Come on, we got to get out there and help him."

"That boy can't keep himself out of trouble for five minutes," Deuce said. "I'm sorry, baby."

Kendall did me the courtesy of not coming out of the stall

so I wouldn't see her in any compromising ways. I replayed everything to Deuce as we dashed through the crowd.

"Oh, he's getting creamed," some guy in the crowd yelled. Normally I could see over crowds, but people were standing on folks' necks trying to see this fight—you would have thought it was a World Championship bout or something. However, when the police raided the joint, bodies blocking our way moved quickly toward all exits. In the mass of confusion I saw a bloody silver knife in the hands of the gang leader. Savoy dropped to her knees and my heart stopped. I couldn't even recognize her brother's face, and knew from the bloodstain on the left side of his belly that the thug's knife had pierced Saxon's stomach. I was so torn I didn't know what to do. I didn't want to let thug dude get away with it. I wanted to go after him, fight a fair fight and kill his behind. He had waited until his boys tore Saxon up and then he took him out—it just wasn't right.

But as soon as I turned, Savoy called out, "Perry, help me! Help me, please. You've got to help me stop the bleeding. My brother, I don't know if he's going to be okay. Please, I'm scared, help me!"

"I'm going to go get the police," Deuce said.

Part of me was wishing I hadn't been such a knucklehead in the beginning—in terms of Savoy—and all of this could have been prevented. But it was facing me now. When I touched Saxon's body he wouldn't even move, scream out in pain, or cry for help. My body started shaking as if I was in an ice cold freezer. It was déjà vu. I remember the paramedics trying to save Collin Cox, our other suitemate. Though his prospects had been bleak, he pulled through. Seeing Saxon's frail body in front of me, I just didn't think that he would be so lucky.

"We're going to lose him," Savoy said, reading my mind.

Instinctively, I said, "No, no. He's going to get through this! He's going to get through this," as I rocked her in my arms.

I was so sick of hospital waiting rooms that if I had stock for every time I had been in one over the past couple of years I'd be rich. It was a good thing we were here for the bowl game, because Savoy's parents were still in Miami and met us at the hospital. I didn't know how to console her. She stayed in the arms of her mom, as her dad and I paced in opposite directions so we would stay clear of one another. I knew deep down it was useless to hold out much hope. Saxon was in real bad shape and if this was the end for him . . . I didn't even know if he was saved, and that killed me. I cried out, *Lord, give me another chance! Help me make sure that my friends know You. You want me to be a fisherman of men, alright. I'll put down my shoulder pads. I'm here. I'm available. Save my friend. Dang, I know we can't do it without You. This is a lot—dealing with trouble.*

~ 3 ~

Clinging to Hope

I was in such a daze, hoping everything would be okay with Saxon, that when my cell phone rang it startled me so that I almost took a leak in my pants.

"There you are, son," my dad said. I hoped he hadn't called the hotel and checked up on me. I had told him and my mom that I was going to go sleep off my depression over the horrible game. Before I could explain the night, he took my breath away by saying, "Son, this isn't good news."

What in the world did he have to tell me? What wasn't good news, what was so bad? With Bilboa's aunt and uncle's accident early in the year, I couldn't take it for granted that just a mere car ride across town would always prove to be a safe one.

"Are you and mom okay?"

He took a deep breath. "It's Grandma."

"What's wrong with your mom?" I said, feeling very angry at the Lord. He told me that he would never put more on me than I could bear. I couldn't bear losing Saxon, and now my dad calls me at 3 AM to talk about my grandma. For real, this is too much.

"Are you at the hotel or not, son? We talked to your coach—he said you could ride back with us. Grandma's at the hospital. We drive back tonight, we'll be back there by midmorning."

"Going back with the team won't be quicker for me?"

"No, Coach said y'all weren't pulling out until about ten."

"Dad, I'm not trying to stress you but I'm not at the hotel."

"Boy, you hooked up with some girl?"

"No sir, I'm at the hospital."

"WHAT!" he exclaimed with such an irate voice the phone dropped out of my hand.

"Alright, we'll find our way to the hospital. Stay there!" he said after I explained everything. "And we'll just make sure Deuce gets all of your stuff on the plane."

"Yeah, yeah, sure. Grandma going to be okay?"

Dad got all choked up, he couldn't even answer me. My mom got on the phone and said, "Son, we'll see you in a little while. We don't know much about your grandmother's situation, other than she had a severe stroke and they've called all the family in."

I sat down in the chair, put my hands over my eyes and wept. What in the world was going on? It wasn't good, it didn't feel right, and I needed comfort. I didn't feel right seeking it from God because I had issues with Him. I had actually forgotten where I was until Savoy came over to me. I teared up when she said to me in a sweet voice, "It's going to be okay. It's not your fault and it's not my fault. We just got mixed up with some horrible people and Saxon is going to be okay. He's going to be alright."

"I hope he will, babe, but it's my grandma—my parents are on their way to get me. She is in a hospital too, in Atlanta."

"Oh, no," she said. "We just got to believe that both of them are going to be okay, Perry. Pray and trust God."

"Whatever," I said to her, really feeling completely frustrated.

I wasn't perfect and I wasn't doing things right. But daggone, a whole lot of crazy negroes are living a life of sin, fattening their pockets, escaping the police and partying with their friends nightly, and never have any kind of drama like I seemed to always find myself in. I saw my parents come in. Not having any news about Saxon or my grandma's condition was unsettling. I couldn't stay; I had to jet. Before leaving, I headed over to Deuce and told him to explain to Coach Red that all of it was my fault.

"It'll be alright, man. Just go with your family. It'll be alright," Deuce told me. But after the day from Hell, how could I believe that I would possibly survive? The anger that I had tried so hard to get rid of was now back. In the car with my parents, I put on my iPod because I didn't want to hear the gospel music my father was playing to try to encourage himself. I just wasn't feeling it. I felt that God was abandoning his promise. Many people I cared about were hurting and it was just taking a lot out of me. When we made it back to the Georgia line, my dad woke me up. I hadn't been with him daily since going off to college, but he still knew me pretty well.

"So, you angry now. Mad at the world, huh? Everybody ain't gon' live, son, if it's Saxon's time to go, if it's my momma's time to go. Though we may not agree with God's plan, He knows better than we do. He knows the way. You've got to let go of the need to know why. When you believe in Him you've got to understand that He owes you no explanation."

"So He just gets to make all of the rules? Though we play the way He tells us to play, He still pulls the rug from under our feet."

"First of all, son, none of us will be perfect until we are with Him. God didn't make you go to either one of those clubs—the one the coach benched your behind for or the one where your friend got stabbed."

I did a double take. I couldn't believe my father was talking so squarely to me. If I didn't respect him I would have taken my fist and punched him so hard his head would have gone through the driver's side of the window.

"Don't be looking at me like I've done lost my mind. I'm telling you what's real. Did He make you go to those clubs? . . . Answer me!" he said when I said nothing. I shook my head. "ANSWER ME!"

"No."

"Alright then. Now my momma, she been prescribing her own stuff, you know what I'm saying? Smoking that stuff, trying to ease her own pain. I don't want her in pain and I don't want her getting high every night trying to alleviate it. It's our time to go when we get tired, we've just got to know that God knows best. We're just supposed to be ready and everybody we know and love is supposed to be ready too, because if that's the case you can face whatever comes and believe that God's got it."

We drove the rest of the way in silence, listening now to his gospel music. He had a point. God didn't leave me when I needed Him. I need not be mad at Him. I needed to find my way back.

•

"So, he's in a coma?" Chaplain Moss asked me as I sat in his office a week later.

"Yeah, I don't understand all of the medical terms and reasons why, but it doesn't look good. They're saying if he comes out of it that he might be on life support or something," I said, trying to shake off the flu-like symptoms that were catching up with me. I'd been on the go every day, driving back and forth to Rockdale County Hospital to see my grandmother. I guess I should be excited because she was released and now resting back at home. I didn't have to feel obligated to go there because my aunts, uncles, cousins, parents, and a ton of her neighbors and church friends, were all there to serve. Deep inside I wished that I could be in Miami and whisper something crazy to Saxon, like, "Man, you ain't no good. I'm a way better baller than you." Something that would just irritate him and make him jump up out of his deep sleep and go off on me.

"So how do you feel about all of this?" C. Moss asked, leaning over his desk, waiting on me to tell the whole truth and nothing but my deep true feelings. I just swallowed hard, wishing my itchy throat away. I reached for a tissue off of his desk.

"I don't know how I feel."

"A lot of mixed emotions?"

"Yeah! Being grateful that my grandmother is going to be okay, I want to scream a big 'Thank You' from Mount Everest to the Lord. Yet how can I, when I am still gloomy because the sparkiest teammate I have might be gone."

"And if he's gone, where do you think he's going?"

"You've never seen him at any of your FCA meetings, have you?" I said, harshly. I was not trying to be funny, rude, mean or any of that. But I didn't have time to be sitting in a counseling session having someone pick me apart when I was broken. I knew I had issues with God. I knew I was mad. Saxon was not a believer—or maybe he was, and the life he led just didn't show it.

"I can't judge Saxon. I don't know," I said to C. Moss.

"Fair. Can you judge yourself?"

I knew where he was going with this whole line of questioning. He wanted to know if I thought I had witnessed enough. If I had led Saxon to Christ and if I had given him the opportunity to hear the gospel. But the answer to all of that was, *no*. I met Saxon after my first day of high school as a senior, with a sea of South Carolina's recruits visiting. His cocky behind made me sick to my stomach and I probably wished him a trip underground, truth be told, but time and circumstances had changed our bond. And if he went to spend all eternity with the devil because I didn't explain to him that there was another way, maybe I didn't deserve to be at the Pearly Gates either.

"You don't have to say anything, Perry. I can tell you hate that you didn't witness to him enough. Let me just let you off the hook—I've witnessed to Saxon. He's heard the gospel. He shoved me off, told me he said all the right things in the correct places he needed to, to let people think he knew the Lord, but in reality he told me he didn't. Hearing that news was so damning, so final, so finite. He's got to pull through this, son. There is absolutely nothing wrong with hoping for another chance to make sure he knows God. Heck, maybe he was just pulling my leg and he already does. I mean, you football players have heard so much that you're the best of the best and that you're the cream of the crop, unlike regular students. Sometimes, most times, you get close-minded."

We ended our talk in prayer and as soon as I got back to my apartment, I didn't have time to chat with Lance and Deuce. One of them had been in the kitchen preparing dinner, and though they had a plate set aside for me, it just wasn't social time for me. I was so mad that I couldn't go see my grandma, because the Peach State, which never gets an ounce of snow, had flurries falling. I called my dad and said, "I'm just gonna come."

"Naw, son, I don't need you on the road. It's really cold, it's icy out there. It's a little bit of rain mixed with that snow. Please stay put. Your grandma's up and she can talk. But I want to warn you—the stroke has affected the appearance of her face. The doctors are saying she's not out of the woods. If you want, you can talk to her for a moment."

"She's awake? Yeah, yeah. Let me talk to her."

"Hey, punkin pie, you've been worried about me, boy?"

"Yes ma'am," I said.

"I heard you every time you came and visited me. I'm always asleep and they only let me have a few visitors up in that little old hospital room, but I know you been there, I seen ya. I'm supposed to be the sick one, but one time I woke up and you were knocked out. I ain't bother you, though. I figured you needed your rest. One of my boyfriends said you were nice at the hospital, signing autographs and stuff. You know that meant a lot to me."

"Grandma, you are crazy!"

"And getting better every day."

"You better be getting better," I told her. "I got to buy you that big old house one day soon—big enough to have your different men in different parts of it, that kind of big."

"Oh, child, please. I don't need to hide nobody. I've been thinking, seeing stuff. I just had to break all of their hearts and had to let them know that I was still in love with my dead husband. I'm real tired, Perry. I know God has got something better for me than all of this."

"But Grandma, you gon' be okay," I urged.

"Yeah, I'ma be alright up in Heaven, boy, and ain't no doubt that's where I'm going—to my momma, my great grandmomma, to see her face who I haven't seen since I was little. Your granddaddy, mm-hmm, he mad that I got a lot of ole men friends, but we'll straighten all of that out when I get up there."

"Grandma, you don't need to talk like that."

"Baby, if you don't remember nothing I done taught you, and I know I done taught you a lot—"

"Yes ma'am, you have."

"—I want you to remember that if you are a believer there ain't nothing wrong with knowing that this place is not your home. Be excited about what's to come. Ain't no need in rushing nothing and I ain't saying—well maybe I am saying.

Whenever the Lord say I'm ready, I'll be ready. Make sure you lay some pretty red roses on my grave now."

I agreed, but her crazy talking was making me more irritable. I really felt sick. I started coughing, my body started aching. Would my life get well?

"So, this is Hotlanta, huh?" my cousin Pillar said as I drove her around downtown. She was something else, a cute mixed girl that knew she had it going on.

"So where you want to go, what you want to see?" I asked her, hoping she had a plan.

"This is your town. Everyone knows who you are and that you're the man in it, wherever."

I turned the car around and headed for the Georgia Aquarium. It was now the largest in the world. Now that I only lived two miles from it on Tech's campus I'd never had a chance to visit. When I pulled up she said sarcastically, "Oh, so you thought I wanted to see some fish?"

I knew she was high maintenance and would insist on telling me where she wanted to go. I stupidly had taken her at her word, and my plan wasn't good enough. I pulled over and said, "Alright, where do you want to go?"

"I thought we could go to Morehouse."

It was so obvious that she wanted to flirt with somebody, but I knew that there was a gate on campus and tricked her and said, "Yeah, we can go to the AU."

"It's called the Atlanta University Center, right?"

"Yep."

"Oh my gosh, this campus is nice," she said, looking at the Spelman campus. "I like Stanford and all, but it's just too rigid. I know I'm half white, but I need some culture, plus I need to get away from my folks. They can just drive up when they want and that just irks me."

"Hey, we can get out and walk. It's cold and there's ice on the ground."

"I just want to go to the admissions office and check out what my options are. Then maybe I can transfer."

Just as we stepped out my phone rang. "Hey mom."

"Hey, where you at sweetie?"

"I'm with Pillar."

"Yeah, her dad told me. I just saw him a moment ago at the hospital."

I sighed. The look of despair on my face made my cousin Pillar ask me, "Cuz, what's wrong?"

I held up one finger to ask her to hold on for a minute, when all of a sudden my mom made me drop to my knees when she said, "Your grandmother is gone."

"It's Grandma."

"Oh no, are you serious? She was okay. I was just with her last night." My cousin started crying and I held her.

"Alright Mom, we'll be out there."

"Aight baby, ain't no need in rushing. She's in a better place."

Here one minute and gone the next. She had just told me she was tired, but I so wished she had gotten a good night's rest and been rejuvenated. However, she took a turn for the worst, having a second stroke that sent her on to glory.

It was actually a great thing. The next several days were so much fun. My family was rejuvenated, we laughed through our tears. Her friends came by and told stories that confirmed my grandma was crazy. She was certainly one of a kind and would definitely be missed, but she knew the Lord and she knew where she was going and she was excited to get there. How could you not be happy? The day of the service Payton and I rode behind our parents.

"I miss you, sis." Understanding that life was precious and

I couldn't take it for granted, I added, "You alright up there in school?"

"Tad and I got issues, women are crazy, the pledging thing is driving me nuts, and I miss my little brother too. I guess life is alright, right?" Payton asked. I nodded.

Feeling like God wanted more from me, I scratched my head and asked, "How do you witness? It seems that telling people about God isn't all that cool. I don't want to push my beliefs on anybody. But with Tad's cousin down . . ."

Payton placed her hand on my shoulder to comfort me. "Yeah, I know, he's still in a coma."

"Yeah, I mean if Grandma was supposed to make it through and she didn't, odds really are that he's gone. I don't know, you know. I just want to do more, you know? For God I can't have any regrets, you know, but a part of me is just . . ." I looked out the window as I couldn't finish my own statement, not wanting to admit I was a little scared to step out there for God.

"You don't want to be ridiculed?"

"Exactly!"

"Well, the word says that if I be lifted up, I will draw all men unto me," my sister said. "I'm not the perfect Christian either. I know my halo is a little tilted, but for the most part I don't let anyone push me into something I don't want to do. If you truly believe in God, then stand for Him, and don't care what anyone else says. Remember, folks talked about Jesus. So who are we that we can't endure for the One who gave His all for us?"

"Right, right," I uttered, agreeing that my sister had a valid point.

"You know Pillar said she's going to go to school here."

"Yeah, we were talking about it when we got the call about Grandma."

"Yeah, well she's been working Uncle Percy for the last

couple of days, and she's serious. She's in Atlanta with you, and as wild as that girl is you're just going to have to decide."

"What do you mean? I can't tell Pillar what to do."

"You have more influence than you think, my brother. When you want to grab that ball that most think is uncatchable you find a way to do it. Use that same logic for stepping up to Christ."

"Will what I say work?"

"You've got to believe it will." I nodded.

The service for my grandmother was a blast. Because she had played the piano for several local choirs, there were eight different churches in the house singing songs of praise. There was no note that I heard that was out of tune and people got up and testified how she impacted their lives. Her nontraditional ways saved a lot of people.

As the preacher preached I envisioned my granddad with his hand extended, and her taking it, and them going off together. I felt myself running after them. "Wait, wait. Don't leave me." And then my granddad turning around and saying, "Hey, we'll see you soon, but you have some things to take care of, and not only on the field. Make me proud and stand up. Be the difference. We're cheering you on up here. Live your life and stop thinking the Lord don't care. Dying when you have a Heavenly home is a good thing, son."

And the next thing I knew my sister was pulling on me so she could be the flower girl and I the pallbearer for my grandmother's precious body. My sister smiled at Tad and I had to blink twice when I saw his cousin, my girl Savoy, there next to him as well.

My sister took my hand and said, "See, it's all good."

I had to admit it felt real good clinging to hope.

~ 4 ~

Recruiting New Ideas

After the celebration of placing my grandmother's precious body in the ground, I couldn't wait to go over to Savoy and give her a huge hug. We both had been going through it. I felt bad that I hadn't talked to her, but the wide smile on her face told me that she understood that I needed time. As much as I needed her arms around me, every step I took closer to her I realized her brother, her twin, would probably have the same ceremony real soon. As sad as I was, grieving, what would I be able to share with her to ease her pain?

"Hey, baby," I said to her, giving her a big hug. She was standing alone, because her cousin Tad had already made his way over to my sister.

"I'm so sorry about your grandmother, but I tell you what, this has been a party!"

"Yeah, she had a lot of people who loved her and will miss her."

"Sounds like she has a lot of friends who have gone on and are welcoming her right now. Y'all were partying down here, but I could feel the spirit letting me know that they were partying up there. You know what I'm saying?"

"Yeah!" I said, really excited, hugging her even tighter. With all she was going through, she was uplifting me, encouraging me. What a great girlfriend. This was a blessing. I looked deep into her eyes, trying to study them and understand her pain. I wanted to be the attentive boyfriend that I had abandoned the last few months. Try to be a brother in Christ as well.

"I can tell you want to ask me about Saxon," she said as she squeezed my hand real tight. It was like she was trying to tell me to get ahold of myself. I squeezed her hand back, letting her know that I was ready for her and that we were going to get through this. And even though I didn't understand what all God did up there, we were going to have to trust Him.

"I feel real bad talking about my brother at your grandmother's funeral, you know?"

"I'm just sorry I haven't been able to sit with you guys in the hospital and stuff."

"No, no. I understand that you had a lot to do, you needed to be with your family. I just didn't want you to be mad at me because I didn't call you with updates," she said.

I didn't want to look at her like she had completely lost her mind, but what update did she need to keep giving me? He was in a coma; doctors had pretty much given up hope. I wasn't interested in hearing about his new bed sores, but I didn't want to seem insensitive so I said, "No, no you didn't have to give me an update. It's fine."

"You and I have been praying and we got a miracle."

"What? What are you talking about?"

Before she could answer, my aunts came over and squeezed my cheeks, my uncles punched me in the arm. Everybody wanted to be introduced to her. Everybody was minding their manners until my crazy cousin Pillar came over and said, "Oh, Perry. She's cute!" Then she turned to Savoy, and said, "Are you going to be able to handle my cousin? All my friends back home want him. The way he's all over ESPN. You gon' be able to handle him, girl?"

I looked at her like, *Alright now, dang! We supposed to be family. Don't sell me down the river like that*. Plus, with Pillar going to school up at Spelman, the last thing she needed to do was alienate my girl, when she was going to be right up the street. But I could tell as Pillar looked Savoy from head to toe she didn't care about making friends. My cousin thought she was all that, and thought I was all that because I was related to her, and didn't care about anyone's hurt feelings. I put my arm around Savoy and said, "Alright, it's good seeing all of y'all. I'ma go talk to my girl. I'll see y'all at the repast."

"Your cousin . . ." Savoy rolled her eyes and couldn't even finish the statement.

"Yeah, I know."

"When is she packing up and going back to California?"

"Well, that's just it."

"What do you mean, that's just it?"

"She's transferring to Spelman."

"Ugghh!" she screamed.

"Seriously, what good news do you have on your brother? They have hope now, they think he might come through? What?"

"Perry, he's completely awake. He came out of his coma, he's great, he's lucid. He knows everybody and he's been in physical therapy for days. It's just remarkable. He has a strong will to do more, be more, have more. They released him. That's why I was able to make it. God spared his life."

Then she hugged me again. We walked over to her car. Tad was going to ride with Payton to the church, and as the wind blew across my face it was like God saying, *See, you doubted me. You wanted more time with him. You wanted more time to tell him about me. Alright my friend, go, get ready to fish. Now that you have a second chance, be fired up.*

I just thought, *Thank you, Lord!* I got into the car and I didn't want to break down in front of my girl. But from being graveside to now knowing that Saxon was okay, that God spared him for a reason, just made me weep. Yeah, I was a man, yeah I was tough, but all that surface stuff took a back seat. Now it was time to be real.

"It's okay," Savoy said, placing her hand on my back. "I knew you cared for Saxon, I just didn't know you cared so much. He's okay, though, and your grandmother is okay too. God does know what He is doing."

She started rubbing on my neck and then she leaned over and kissed my cheek. Her hands cupped my face. We felt the joy about what was going on in our lives, the emotion of the moment, and we kissed. Our tongues connected and then I felt conflicted. God was hearing my prayer. I didn't want my grandmother to be in pain anymore. I wanted another chance with Saxon. He was alive, yet I couldn't follow his way. I pulled back.

"I'm sorry, I shouldn't have done that."

"No, me either. We've got to find another way to express our feelings to one another."

"We've got to honor God in this thing," I said.

Unable to forget how good her kiss felt, I sure hoped we could.

"Dang, it seems like I ain't never gon' catch Saxon up," I said as I slammed the door to my apartment. It was now mid-February, and Saxon had officially been back on campus for a week. Every time I'd go by his place one of his suitemates would say that I'd either just missed him, or that he was asleep, or that he was just too tired for company. At first I took it at face value, but as I got more and more of the brush-off I really wondered what the avoidance was all about.

"Have y'all seen him?" I asked Lance and Deuce. The two of them turned around like they didn't want to answer me or something. I wasn't a kid, my feelings weren't going to be hurt—either they had or hadn't seen him. So I asked again with real force. "Have you seen Sax or not? What's the big deal?"

"We've seen him, man, alright," Lance said.

"Well, why do I have the feeling that you two guys know more than you're telling me?"

"I don't want to get into it," Deuce said, trying to walk to his room.

"Unh uh," I said to him, yanking on his sweater. "Talk to me. This ain't cool, man. If you know something, let me know."

Lance then took it upon himself to walk toward his room. I wasn't an idiot; I could figure it out, but in our house we had a bond—they were supposed to tell me the rough stuff without feeling uncomfortable.

"Alright guys, come on back in here. Let's talk."

"Alright, alright. He's really upset with you. Pissed off, man. Like angry, angry, angry."

"Dang, Lance, man. You got a big mouth," Deuce said, throwing a pillow from the couch across the room.

"Yeah right, he would have kept badgering us until we said something."

"I'm sure this is just temporary," Deuce said, placing his hand on my shoulder.

"I tried to tell him that you weren't at fault, but he wasn't hearing me. He doesn't remember everything exact, but what he does remember, he thinks you punked him."

"Is he over there right now?" I said, heading toward the front door.

"Naw, naw man. You can't go right over there and tell him we told you," Deuce said, standing in my way. "He just got out of the hospital, just respect his wishes. Let his memory clear up and he'll get over all of this."

"As worried as I was about this joker, I really feel like I got a mission to go over there and talk to him. He's going to hear what I have to say and if he's ticked with me he needs to open his mouth and say something."

I pushed Deuce to the side, walked across the hall and banged on the door as hard as I could, and as I waited for someone to open, I thought, *Devil, you are a trip. As heavy as Saxon has been on my mind in trying to talk to him about God and all that, and I would be the one that he didn't want to see. Devil, you have no power here.*

"Saxon, open up the door, man. Now, man. It's Perry, man, I need to talk to you now." But he wouldn't come to the door. "It's about Savoy, open up! Hurry up! Open up!"

I couldn't believe I was making up, but I knew if he was in there and he heard his sister's name or if I alluded to anything like that he'd be running to see me, and I was correct. The door opened and I saw his face.

"What? What's up with my sister?" Saxon said with an attitude. I pushed past him and walked inside.

"Man, your sister's fine."

"Skky, I ain't never known you to be a liar."

"I ain't never known you to be a coward," I said back to him.

"A coward? What, me? Man, please, I ain't the one that ditched the fight. You couldn't even stand up for my sister's honor, to make sure that she didn't get violated, and you turn and leave me by myself to get jumped on and stomped on. I was in a coma because of you. Now you've got the nerve to show your face to me?"

"I was told that you didn't even remember a lot of what

happened that night. So whoever pieced all that together for you missed out on a lot."

"Please, I already took you for a high-class brown-noser." Saxon went back over to the door and opened it for me.

Because Savoy and I felt uncomfortable about our last encounter, we kept a good amount of distance between us. We talked on the phone, but those chats were quick checkups, nothing deep. She and I hadn't really talked about why I wasn't right beside her brother when it happened. Had Saxon gotten into her mind and warped it too?

"Get out, Skky, seriously. I'm tired, get out."

"I'll leave, but you're going to hear me out," I said, walking over to the door and shutting it.

"Alright, what? What do you have to say? Hurry up."

"That night I was about to go get your sister when you jerked me back and told me you had it. I went to find Deuce for back-up. Everything happened so fast. With the big crowd, we couldn't easily get to you. It wasn't about lack of trying or caring or not wanting to be there. I was a part of the paramedics being called. I did not flee anything. I was with your sister, and as I took each breath for those first few days I thought about it over and over and over again. I prayed for you. And when they said it looked bleak for you I grieved, man. Wishing, hoping, and just trying to trust God that He would give you another chance."

"Another chance for what?"

"For me to ask you, are you saved?"

"A month of my life is gone, man, from me trying to protect my sister. There is no need in trying to get me to be some Holy Ghost–filled whacko. I'm alive because I kept pushing and I wanted to be here. I'm sick of you and my sister trying to make me believe otherwise. Sell that God nonsense to some other fool. I ain't buying it."

I shrugged and turned around and opened the door, but

this time I was on the outside. I looked down and thought, *Devil, you might have won the battle, but you ain't winning the war.*

"I'm sorry this isn't the ideal date," I said to Savoy as we went out on Valentine's Day. She was looking out the window of my car, with her lips pouted like the day was messed up because I hadn't presented her with flowers or her gift. But shoot, I had forgotten about all of that. Although it was a last minute thing for me, I was excited about us being together. Both of us had had a real rocky start to this year.

"I said I was sorry," I said to her, trying to get her attention.

"It's alright, it's alright. What do you want me to say, that I am excited about going to the Varsity to meet some recruit? Either he's going to come to Tech or he's not. Why you have to babysit on Valentine's Day is crazy. And then to go to dinner with the chaplain and his wife—I know we need to figure out a way to not be all over each other, but I ain't trying to get counseling. This should be romantic. You're going from babysitting somebody to someone babysitting us. Forgive me for not jumping up and down with excitement."

She had a point. I couldn't do anything about the recruit; Coach said it was our turn to hang out with the prospective player. We had no say in it. "It's only going to be a few minutes. We're just going to have dinner with the guy and answer any questions that he has about Tech, and then we're out of there. Plus I didn't expect you to eat at the Varsity. Sorry you don't think that going over to Coach Moss' would be nice, but he invited us. I thought it would be a great insight into what we want to do. After all, you haven't really talked to me lately."

"Aw, Perry, don't even use that as an excuse. You haven't

talked to me either. My brother's not just mad at you anyway. He's mad at me too. So, if you're taking it out on me that he has an attitude with you, it's not fair."

"No, no. Where are you even getting that from?" I asked, really frustrated how our night was kicking off.

We got to the Varsity and it was really crowded. Everyone was looking for a cheap date, but the Varsity was a historic place known for great hotdogs, hamburgers and chili cheese. The place was smelling so good, but I couldn't be tempted. I couldn't go to Coach Moss' house with a full stomach. I had the name of the recruit and I was supposed to meet him at the door at six. Six-fifteen came and I couldn't find him.

I said to Savoy, "I'm just gon' walk around, I'll be right back."

"That's cool," she said, still a little salty about earlier. I wasn't gone for two minutes when I heard Savoy scream out, "Don't touch me! Get your hands off of me!"

I rushed to the back side of the building and found Savoy moving away from this young, buff dude who fit the description of the recruit.

"Are you Jeff Wade?"

"Yeah, man. Chick is trippin'."

"Yeah right. You felt me up and said a little bit more than that. I can't deal with this, Perry," she said, coming over to me.

"I ain't do none of that."

"You are going to believe him over me?" she asked.

I was so torn; I knew she was a little paranoid from everything that happened at the beginning of the year at the club. Maybe she was on her cycle or something, because she had an attitude with me all the way over here. Or did I really need to take in what she said and deal with this chump for being too forward with my girl? Quickly I thought of my options. If

I jumped on him I could possibly be arrested and be in the newspaper again for some foolishness. He could tell Coach, he could probably go to another school. Talk about a recruiting trip gone bad. But if I didn't, I could lose my girl with her thinking that I really didn't have her back. I didn't want our relationship to be built on lies—we needed trust. She needed to know that I would be there for her, and with her brother accusing me of bailing during his fight, that's the last thing I wanted on my conscience. So I thought about it for real. I prayed, *Alright Lord.* Savoy stood with her hands on her hips and her head rolling, waiting on me to do something. Jeff had his hands folded like he was the best recruit in America and I had better not do anything to jeopardize it. *Can you give me some insight Lord; can you help me out here?* I pointed one finger to Jeff and put my arm around Savoy and said, "Let me deal with this, man."

Jeff nodded. "Cool. I'ma step in and grab a lil' something to eat."

As soon as we were alone, Savoy grabbed my shirt and passionately said, "You do believe me, right? Why didn't you say anything?"

"I have to deal with this the right way, and he is a recruit for the school. I'm not going to tolerate his actions toward you but I can't just go off on him in public, you know? When we tell Coach that recruits are not of good character, Coach backs off of them anyway. We're a class act school. It's not about just throwing the ball down the field. If we get this guy it could be a big deal, but let me go about it the right way. Can you trust me to do that, baby? I mean I am sorry that our date started out on the wrong note, but I'll make it up to you." I kissed her cheek and put her in the car.

I went inside.

"Alright man, what's up? You hitting on my girl, man?"

Jeff gave me a smug look. “She’s fine, man. I had to touch.”

“I understand, but you can’t be touching up on women like that.”

“I mean it was just a little tap.”

He admitted to me what he had done. I had come at him the right way. I had figured him out.

“I didn’t know she was your girl anyway.”

“Yeah, but you come to Tech or any school really pushing your weight on these females and you’ll get yourself into all kinds of trouble. Besides, my girl has had a lot to deal with. I can’t have anyone messing with her.”

“Aw snap, my bad. Your girl is the one whose brother is on the team, too? Some gang guy messed him up?”

“Yeah, all that.”

“I’ma go apologize. Naw man, that’s cool, let’s just talk about Tech for a little bit. Some of the other guys are going to come and swoop me up. Show me around A-town.”

“Alright, let’s get you a burger.”

“Cool.”

An hour later I was sitting with C. Moss. Savoy was with his wife.

“It’s just hard to get this dating thing right. She has such high expectations and sometimes my motives are so impure. It’s like I can’t be with her, but it’s too hard to be without her. I just don’t know where we fit in. If it’s in the cards for us at all. I think I did the wrong thing by bringing her here for Valentine’s. She’s really ticked at me.”

“There’s nothing wrong with thinking outside of the box and making sure that y’all don’t cross any lines that y’all don’t need to. You know what I’m saying,” he said to me.

“Yeah, I got you.”

“There’s no need to reinvent the wheel either. Just keep

God in prayer, get on out of here and take her to a movie or something. You can finish the night doing something that makes her excited. Stay on your prayers and the Lord will continue to show you where to lead in this dating relationship. You'll figure it out, stay open. There's nothing wrong with recruiting new ideas."

~ 5 ~

Showing True Feelings

"I'm sorry, can you forgive me?" Savoy said to me as we left the Moss' home after dinner. Because her attitude had been chillier than the February air, I was taken aback that she was apologizing, and honestly I didn't know what exactly she was seeking forgiveness for. There was a grocery store nearby so instead of driving right to the movie theater to see a romantic movie to salvage our Valentine's evening, I pulled into the parking lot. I figured we needed to talk and I wanted to look directly into her eyes and listen to what she had to say and speak from my heart.

"I've been angry at God!" she said to me.

Wow, I thought. She was one of the most solid Christians I knew.

"Yes, He saved my brother. Yes, He put us back together and yes I should love Him just because He's God, but I've been really upset with Him. Because I am upset with Him I have been mad at the world, particularly you."

"So do you feel like your brother, that I let you down after the big game?"

"No, you explained everything that happened and it makes complete sense and I can't blame you for any of that anyway. You know I blamed myself for trying to make you jealous. And I guess that is just it. I guess what makes me so angry is that as much as I prayed to the Lord to have Him try and help me stay on the right path things come up, and it's like Satan is able to come in my mind and corrode it. I feel like frazzled wires connected to nothing, and every time I try to tell my brother about God he says so many other things that make me doubt salvation is real, and that scares me. I just found out that my dad's sister, Tad's mom—"

"Yeah," I said.

"—She has cancer," Savoy told me with teary eyes.

"Oh man, are you serious? I hadn't even talked to Payton."

"I'm sure she knows because Tad is real torn up about it. We sort of just found out but I don't think she has long to live."

And all of the things that I really felt to tell her—it's okay, this is not where we are supposed to be, that we live here to get to Heaven, that God is going to take care of us, that it's all going to be fine—I'm not sure of it myself. Some mornings are shaky, just thinking about my body being underground in some box that I can't get out of.

"I'm just afraid. The Lord is not giving me any comfort or any answers and if He was really real don't you think I'd have peace?"

I hugged her, I really appreciated her being vulnerable and sharing her concerns with me. I didn't know if I had the answers that she was looking for but I did know that I truly understood where she was coming from. I mean, not too long ago I was questioning my own salvation, battling with God for the things I felt He wasn't doing right. Thankfully He brought me to a place of comfort, because I had to just trust and have faith and believe.

"That's Satan trying to mess you up, Savoy. That's Satan trying to get into your mind to make you think that all you know to be true is a lie. He's the one who's a liar, call him on the carpet, speak the word. Satan cannot touch or destroy you; you have the protection of the Almighty."

"Why does it feel like everybody that I love is suffering—you with your grandmother, my brother with his life, and my aunt with cancer. I just, I just don't know."

"I don't know a lot, Savoy," I said, holding her hand, "but I do know that the word says to be absent of the body is to be present with the Lord, and my mind can't even conceive what He has in store for us in Heaven and I want to be there. I want to see my grandparents, I want to see my Savior face to face, and I want to hear him say, 'Job well done.' And I know I haven't been living a life that, if He took me right now, He would want to reward me for, but I know that I am alive today and I can do better than I did yesterday. And I know that it is tough to witness to people but that doesn't mean that we are supposed to give up."

"Yeah, but what are we supposed to do? They say so many things about Him not being real that you question yourself."

"You have to trust and believe," I told her. "You've got to stand just as firm as they are. It's like planting seeds in soil and watering them. I mean a seed doesn't automatically become a full bloom. It comes in stages, so who knows what stage you are in at helping people grow in Christ. We want to see them automatically grow up and be some pretty flower, but they might just be a seed, it might be the first time they ever heard the gospel."

"Here I am supposed to be the water of what someone else has said."

"You might be the sunshine that gives them hope that God cares."

"I don't know what stage this is but I will not know all the answers until I am with Him." She got out of the car and walked into the wind. I turned off the car, got out and went over to her.

"I care about you a lot, and me and you have got some issues but that doesn't mean that I am going to give up. That doesn't mean that I am going to stop striving to work this thing out. I know it's harder for me when you're not around, girl, but to get this thing worked out I am surely going to try. We just got to keep going through it, keep praying for each other. Some days I'll be stronger than you, some days you'll be stronger than me."

"So, you're committed to us for real?" she asked, looking at me with the most precious eyes I had ever seen.

"Yeah!" I said from the heart. "I really want you to have my heart, but we're young you know, and just because I don't give you everything you're looking for doesn't mean I'm not giving you all that I've got."

She put her arms around me and squeezed real tight. What we had may not have been perfect but it was real good. Salvation was secure. Our witnessing could be stronger, but because we wanted it to grow we were in a good place. We were real secure and that was awesome.

"Perry, man, come here. Come here," I heard a voice call out as I was about to enter the football complex. "Come on man, don't front and act like you don't know me, dang."

I looked to my left and I looked to my right and all I saw was a bum on the street. As the dingy person walked toward me I swallowed hard. It was Mario, our former quarterback, truly looking like he was strung out on something. If you don't have anything good to say you're not supposed to say anything, right. Well, the guy knew me too well to think that I would be cool with the image before me. I had to be honest, I had to ask what was up. "Man, what's been up with you, why do you look like crap?"

He couldn't even get his words out—he started stuttering

and stumbling. He clearly was high. "Perry, man. I need, I need some money. I need some cash, come on. Give me what you got," he said as he approached me and started looking for my wallet, digging in my pockets.

"Aw man, Mario. Back up, man."

I was stuck between a rock and a hard place for a lot of reasons. One was that I needed to hurry up and get into Coach Moss' office. We were about to head out on a mission trip to the children's hospital. I also couldn't give him any money—clearly he wouldn't be buying any gas or food with it, and I surely didn't want to give him anything that could be a catalyst into anything that could do him more harm.

"Man, I ain't got anything."

"Come on, rich boy, lie to somebody who don't know you. I been waiting on you to come up here. I just need a little twenty or forty, whatever you got I need it. Alright man, come on come on."

I put my hands up in the air and said, "For real, nothing."

Then he turned a little violent and grabbed my collar and said, "It's your fault that I'm in this predicament anyway. You snooped and found out what I was doing. I got messed up, kicked out of Tech, beat up more times than I know. I'ma have to make it anyway, I know how then. You don't want to give a brother a handout."

Maybe I was misjudging him, I mean the more he talked the more he was able to put his words together and sound articulate. I always had a little stash in my dashboard so I told him to hold on, went back to my car and gave him a fifty.

"Thanks man, thanks!" When I got inside C. Moss lit into me.

"You said you wanted to be one of my leaders, Perry. I took that seriously and you come in here late and all when you know we have to be at the hospital at a certain time. We were waiting on you; your tardiness shows no leadership skills. You didn't have the decency to call. I'm not trying to push you out there to do public service—that needs to be something you desire from the heart. You told me you were up to it and now you're dropping the ball. I mean I assume that's not like you. What's up with that?"

I didn't want to laugh because that would have been totally rude, but when I looked up I saw my roommates Deuce and Lance standing behind Coach Moss, where he couldn't see their faces, and they were doing everything but keeping me straight; googling their eyes, sticking fingers up behind his head, just being jerks. Finally I couldn't hold it in and I just bust out laughing. He turned around quickly and caught the two of them being silly and I lost it even more.

"See, you guys just don't understand. When we get to where we're going and you see these kids lying there you won't have such a careless attitude."

"Look Coach, I'm sorry. I'm sorry. They were being . . ."

"No need to apologize. I mean Perry, you're grown, do what you want to do. I'm just letting you know that I didn't appreciate it. It's my job to give and give and pour into you guys. But it is not a part of my job description to put up with your lack of respect." He went around me and went to his car.

"Y'all need to hurry up," he said to everyone without looking back.

"We knew you would be on time, so we were late," Deuce said to me.

"Why were y'all late?"

"You know Lance was hungry."

"I had to get a snack from the cafeteria. You know we going to the hospital and it don't smell right in there. I wanted to be full. Aren't we supposed to bring flowers to the sick and shut-in?" Lance joked.

On the way over Coach Moss remained distant. I did feel bad about letting him down and I did want to tell him what I thought about Mario, because I wasn't sure but it could have been a whole lot more of a big deal. I knew I just needed to pray for Mario. When we got to the hospital the three of us were talking loud, not intentionally. Just three guys joking.

"Shh!" the chaplain said harshly. We could tell by his demeanor that if he had a switch we would get a whooping.

"I hate hospitals," Lance said.

"I'm not too fond of them either," Deuce chimed in. I didn't say a word but concurred with the both of them.

"Well, you get in front since you don't have a problem with it," Lance said, taking my moment of silence as a sign of toughness. At first it was okay. We visited a few kids that were on IVs, we said the right things we needed to say to them, signed some autographs and we were out. No emotional attachment—nothing really big. They had a virus, they took some medicine, and they would be out in a few days. But it wasn't until we got to the cancer ward that both my roommates lost it. There was this one little girl, bald and pale as could be, with this cute little picture of her beside her bed. She used to have long blond hair.

"The football players are here, Mom, the football boys. I love Buzz," the little girl said.

Buzz was our mascot and one of the pictures we had of him was already signed. As I turned and saw my guys tear up, I gave her the picture and a hug, after her mom said it was okay. I held it together until I got to the burn unit and I saw this little boy with only one finger remaining on his left hand from a horrible fire, where we heard he lost two of his siblings. He was twelve and he had been home alone cooking.

"I was going to play football this year in the seventh grade. I don't think I'll be able to play anymore. I'm sad about that."

I was sad about it too, and my heart was breaking. As I

began to break down he reached for my hand with that one little finger and said, "But you know what's going to bring me joy?"

I looked up with eyes full of tears.

"Being able to see you play. I still have my eyes. I can still see. Get out there and play for me next year, you're real bad." When I walked out of the room I just fell to my knees. I was a part of a fallen world. Man wasn't perfect and we needed a perfect Savior to rescue us. The tears kept flowing worse than a raging river, and that made me want to be about God's business. People were hurting, even innocent children, but there was a God who was capable of drying all our tears. When my roommates came over and hugged me it was like feeling an embrace from God. Though I couldn't see it He had all the babies in this place.

Being a big football player, it was sometimes hard to be vulnerable and show your true emotions. A group of us from Tech and other schools went to a college retreat at Lake Lanier, Georgia. The ACC and SEC chaplains sponsored the event to encourage athletes. Though Savoy had come as well, we were hanging in different groups. Being up there to focus on God helped me feel better than I had in a while. It was praise and worship time; ironically, my sister and Lance's sister were up there too, doing some kind of duet. They sounded like angels though. As I lifted my hands to the sky I just wanted to connect with God. I wanted Him to know how much I loved Him. I wanted Him to know out of all of what He was doing for me, if He did nothing else I was determined to be satisfied. Then the Clemson chaplain came up and preached. His message was real convincing.

He said, "Yeah, it's easy for you to be all hyped up about the Lord right now, this is a mountain-top experience. Everything is good, but what happens when you go back to the valley of life? When the classwork is too hard, when you get injured, when the coach benches you, or when the fans aren't on your side? When you have problems with your parents, when you don't have enough money to support some of the extra things you want—what happens when you go back to the valley? Will you be able to live for Christ at that moment?"

I sat there listening, just thinking about his question. I couldn't say for sure that I would, because there had been plenty of times before that I felt charged, that I felt excited about being a Christian, that I promised God that I would do what was right. Then the first opportunity that I had to falter, I fell off, and the consequences that I suffered were a result of bad choices that taught me that I didn't want to go that way again. I wanted to be better. I wanted to make God proud, I wanted to be victorious.

"So, you might be here thinking, so okay, this is going to be hard; hard when the challenges come, hard to live up to the Lord's standards when peer pressure hits. What are you going to do when that girl whispers in your ear, fellas? Ladies, what are you going to do when that guy starts to rub all over those pretty legs? I'm keeping it real with you guys because the real temptations do come, and if you are not mentally prepared before the storm there is no way that you are going to survive during it. You know, it's like down in Florida during hurricane season, if the boards aren't up on the windows or if the folks don't have their supplies stocked or if they haven't left when that heavy tumultuous rain ushers its way into their city, destroying everything in the storm's path. What if the people there aren't prepared? They perish. Well, we're up here today with you guys, filling you up with energy that can hopefully prepare you for what's ahead."

Deuce hit my arm and said, "Dang, man, am I going to be able to set the bottle down now and leave it alone for real?"

"You can do it, man," I looked over and said to him.

The Clemson chaplain continued, "In order to be victorious in Christ you must seek Him and not be afraid that you are His child, let everyone know that you love Him—and a lot of people won't even let you try. 'Naw, I can't mess with so and so. He trying to be a good boy.' See, folks don't want to mess with God, you know? The devil particularly, but when you hide your faith and you don't let anyone know that you are a believer, when you won't even say that you love God, that's when the devil knows that you are not that strong. You'll be easily tempted by the first little carrot he dangles in your face. When you're feeling sad, fall on your knees and tell Him you need Him, when you're feeling excited raise your hands up and let Him know that you are praising Him. Whatever is going on inside of you, let it out. Let God love you. He can only do with you what you will let Him do through you."

"Wow," I said, feeling like someone had given me the key I needed. I couldn't wait to get back and just try it. My salvation had nothing to do with no one else and I couldn't be ashamed of the gospel. I had to proclaim it with every ounce of my being. Lift God up and let Him draw them in. Yeah, I was ready. I hadn't spent much time with Savoy, and she was up at Lake Lanier also. It was such a romantic place during the winter time, the breeze . . . It was a good place and a good time for showing true feelings.

~ 6 ~

Following the Soul

I was so busy that weekend that I hadn't spent that much time with Savoy. She was up at the Lake Lanier conference center as well, and I had just missed her. We had different sessions for the guys and the girls, but now it was time to go back to the central gathering area. I missed her, and it was now time to see if she had gotten as much out of the weekend as I had. On my way to where the girls were hanging out, before I could turn the corner I saw her back, and it looked like two girls were grilling her or something. *What is all of this about?* I wondered.

Then the tall girl said, "I mean we just want to know, not trying to get into your business or anything, we hear you're the one dating Perry Skky Jr. He's fine. Is it true or not?"

"I told you girl, it can't be true," the other one said before Savoy could talk. "If they were dating we would have seen them together, so you wouldn't mind if we gave him a try, right?"

I braced myself because I didn't know how my girl was going to respond and I certainly didn't want her to break down in tears and become all insecure again, like I was going to do her wrong or something. I simply prayed, *Help her, Lord.*

Then to my surprise Savoy said, "You can go for it, he should be coming through sometime soon. I know we came up together and we're heading out together."

"See," the shorter one said, "she's not dating him. She wouldn't have thrown him off on somebody else."

"Oh, I'm not throwing him off on anybody else. I want to be clear that he is my boyfriend, but we're here to praise God and I'm not trying to be with him all this weekend. He was doing his thing and I was doing mine. I thought we all came up here to get closer to God, but y'all talking about coming up here and dating somebody else's man. I'm not trying to say what you did and did not get out of the weekend, but it seems like you might want to rethink that thought. I don't have Perry on a leash if he has feelings about wanting to be with someone else. No, go for it."

That was my cue to make her feel more than sure that I was committed to her. I came around the corner, took her hand, pulled her to me and gave her a nice kiss.

"Sorry to be rude, girls, but I was just trying to give my girl some affection. I missed her this weekend." After we came out of our embrace, I said, "Oh, I'm Perry Skky, her boyfriend. You ready to go?"

She just grinned from ear to ear and I liked that look. We were connected. She wasn't sure if I had overheard her or if I just knew what she needed, but either way it was right on time and that was a God thing. She was right, this weekend had been about us getting closer and I think we had done that. We were able to connect better with one another. What a great relationship.

"Hey, man," Deuce said, "Mario's out there to see you."

"What man, are you serious?"

It was eleven o'clock at night, I just finished studying for a major test, and all I wanted to do was crash.

"Man, he looks spaced out. Seriously, I think you need to talk to him."

"I wouldn't go nowhere with Mario," Lance said, eavesdropping on the conversation though he was supposed to be minding his own business fixing a sandwich or something. "What? Don't look at me like that. The guys he messes with are crazy. I still remember the beat down they gave me."

"How you know he even want something like that? I saw him last week and he asked me for some change," Deuce confessed.

"Well, he already hit me up for some too," Lance said. "I wish I would have known he had gotten some from you."

"Wait, both of y'all gave him some money? I already gave him some too."

"I already knew when I gave him some what he was into, but he made me feel bad for me having his job," Lance said.

"He made me feel bad too," Deuce admitted, "saying us brothers got to stick together. Yeah he played on my heart strings too."

We heard the door get a good pounding.

"Well, you better go on and get on out there," Deuce said.

"I'm out of change."

"Yeah, take your wallet." Lance threw my wallet over from the counter to me.

"Ha, ha, ha. Y'all been giving him that little hustle. I've given him some real money, and I'm not paying him any more."

"You say that," Lance said. "You're such a wuss. He'll talk you out of your shirt."

"Perry, open up. Open up."

I grabbed my keys and headed to the door.

"Mario, man. What's up guy?" I said, trying to keep the conversation light.

"Perry, I need your help. I really do." I thought he looked bad the first time I saw him, but he looked even worse now.

"Man, I'm tired. I got a big test coming up. I got to go to bed, Mario."

"I just need your help, you can't leave me out there."

"I don't have no money."

"I don't want money, I need you to help me."

"Help you with what?" I asked.

"I've been doing drugs; don't judge me, man."

"Naw man, I ain't gon' judge you."

"I need to go to this group, see. They'll—they'll help me, and I need to make sure I do it and stuff, and I just need you to go. I don't have anybody to help me like that, anybody who cares, and see I know you do. You, you told me I could do this and that it was hard."

"Okay, okay man. Alright."

"I need to get dropped off, my car, I don't . . . I don't really have a car anymore. I had to sell it because . . . um because."

"Okay, I got my keys right here. Where are we going?"

"My bag and stuff is downstairs, it's . . . it's under my car."

"I thought you didn't have . . . you said your car wasn't working."

"I know—just help me, okay?"

"Well, why don't you spend the night here and I take you in the morning?"

"NO, no! It's got to be done now," he said, grabbing my arm and jerking me.

I wasn't really sure what was going on with him. Taking him to a facility where he could detox seemed like something I was down to do. True, in an ideal world it would be great to do it the next day, but if he was that determined to go get help, that urgent, I had to do everything in my power to stand beside him, get him there and push him through the door. I didn't know how addicted he was, but I was sure excited to hear him say that he wanted to get some help. When we got down to my car he asked me to open my trunk. I was down with helping him move some of his stuff but he was very firm and determined.

"I can drive, too, since I know where I'm going."

"Man, please. I don't even think you can walk a straight line let alone drive my car. Man, please."

"Alright, alright."

I didn't know much about the Southside of Atlanta. I knew it was an area that I didn't want to get caught in at night. I wasn't saying I was afraid of somebody jumping me, but I mean, it just wasn't smart for me to be out riding in a sort of flashy car up and down the projects.

"Where is this place?" I asked him as we drove through some apartment complexes that looked abandoned.

"It's . . . it's just up a little bit. See, I got to go get some more of my stuff."

"So . . . Wait a minute, wait a minute. Where are we going? Don't give me no bull. Don't feed me no junk. I'm supposed to be taking you to some house and . . . what you trying to get me involved in?"

"I'm just picking . . . I'm just picking up something. Come on Perry. Alright, it's this house here, pop the trunk."

Already there, I was just pissed. I popped the trunk and sat there as he jumped out, grabbed the bag and went up to the house. It was the weirdest thing to me—if he was going to pick something up, why in the heck did he have to take a full bag inside? Yeah, something wasn't right and before I could start up my car and leave I heard the police say, "Freeze. Get out of the car, man, get out of the car. Get out right now."

I got out of the car with my hands in the air and was forced to the ground. Angry as could be, I wondered why in the world I let my gut allow me to follow Mario in the first place. Could I get out of this? Because whatever this was, it was a mess.

"Okay, get him out of here," a guy sounding like he was in charge said to the two cops that were holding me. They shoved me into a police car and drove around the corner. The next thing I knew we had stopped. Not like they were taking me to the police precinct, not like they were reading me my rights, it just seemed unorthodox. I was a football player, not a detective, but I was smart enough to know they weren't going about everything the right way.

"Hey, I get a phone call or something," I yelled out. My cell phone was in my pocket. If I needed to push PLAY and record everything that was going on I was willing to do it. I was not going to be abused.

"Alright, listen. We've been following Mario Shruggs for quite a while. We're not here after you, but we'll prosecute if you don't cooperate." The heftier guy leaned forward and continued, "So, you need to tell us everything you know, young man. You got a bright future over there at Tech."

No one pushed me, but I felt a severe kick right in the bottom of my belly. It was decision time. Mario had gotten me in a mess larger than six pounds of dog poop, but I wasn't a snitch. I just didn't feel right telling them everything that I knew to send him to jail, but could I afford to throw away my future to stand up for somebody who tricked me in the first place? Mario wasn't looking out for me. *Lord*, I prayed, *Tell me what to do here. Give me guidance. Help me see clearly what's right. You lead. I don't want to be too hasty in my thoughts; saying the wrong thing, thinking the wrong thing, messing all of this up. I mean, I'm in handcuffs.* Being in handcuffs was a true awakening. I now needed to stop trying to cover for a friend and be a friend to myself. Besides, if

Mario couldn't see he was doing bad, then I needed to cooperate with the cops and get him off his own dangerous path.

"What's it going to be, Skky? Are you off to jail, son, or do you have something to tell us?"

Knowing that I knew what to do, I was still having trouble opening my mouth and telling all, so I stalled. Looking up, looking down, taking a deep breath.

Then the bigger one of the cops said, "Alright, let's take him downtown."

"Alright, alright," I said.

"We just want to know how you got caught up in this? His car broke down and the next thing you know he's at Tech and you're chauffeuring him around to sell drugs?"

"Hey, wait a minute. Mario told me that I was taking him to a house that detoxed. He said he wanted to get clean. My roommates can attest that he asked for my help, and not to deliver illegal substances to anybody."

"Well, he's getting arrested once he comes out of the house. We just had to catch him in the act of making the sell. He has got so much on him, the problem is that he is not the big fish we're after. Just like we could see that you had a little hesitancy to come clean and let us know what all was going on, we know he will too."

"So, can I go now?"

"No, son, it's not that easy. We need you to go back into the car and wait till he comes out and sees you. He's going to head towards you and then we'll swarm him."

"Lead my friend to the cops? Come on, man."

"If it went down the way you said it did, he ain't no friend of yours, right?"

"He's just a little messed up, that's all."

Fifteen minutes later I was back in my ride with a walkie talkie that the police had given me. They were talking to me through it. "Okay, sit still as if nothing's happening. Don't panic."

I felt like I was selling my friend out, but it was best. Why did having to do the right thing suck sometimes.

"Okay, the door's opening," one of the cops said.

Mario peered out of the door like someone else might jump him and then he tipped his hat to me and came out with the same bag. As he walked toward me, smiling and mouthing the words *I'm sorry*, I wondered when in the world they were going to step in and get him, but he opened up the car door without interference and said, "Man, I'm sorry it took so long."

"Dang, dog." I looked around.

"What you looking around for? I'm here now. Did anybody mess with you?"

Then I realized what the cops were doing. They were really trying to make sure that I wasn't in on this crap. They were able to hear everything that we were saying. It wasn't enough to clear my name, I actually had to incriminate my boy.

"Man, you said you had to pick up something. Why did you take the bag out?"

"Aw man, it's late. I needed to . . . you know, you know . . . I'ma go to the house. Don't worry, I'ma have you back at your place in no time. It took all that time to put my stuff together but you know umm . . . the house is . . . it's right around the corner."

"So, all you wanted me to do was take you somewhere to get you clean?"

"Yeah, man, why are you asking me so many questions, you already know that."

"So you ain't bringing me into nothing shady?"

"Man, please. I wouldn't drag your goody-two-shoes behind into nothing, you'd mess it up. What's with the twenty questions, can we just go?"

Before I could move the car into drive, cops swarmed us.

"What, what dog? You set me up! You set me up?" he yelled.

The larger cop who had talked to me earlier said, "No, you messed this up yourself. Your friend is saving you."

"How's he saving me? You ain't right Perry, you ain't no good man!"

"How you gon' lie to me Mario? You telling me one thing, got me helping you deliver drugs—are you crazy, man? If you don't care about your future, I care about mine."

"You just gon' sell me down the river like that?"

The cops tugged him away; the cop in charge came over and said, "Thanks, I know that must have been hard. We're sorry we left you in it for a while but we just needed to make sure everything was good."

"Yeah, I sort of figured." Not happy at all.

"We're going to let you go, young man, but by no means are you clear of this whole thing. You were using your car to transport drugs."

"Yeah, but you caught it on tape that I didn't know anything about that."

"That is true, but I am saying that you are still a person of interest in a larger investigation. If we have to call you in, for instance, we expect you to comply. You've got too much to lose; you said it yourself. You're doing the right thing." When he placed his hand on my shoulder, I wanted to jerk away. As hard as it was for me I did the right thing, even as I saw Mario getting pulled off in the cop car. This was hard, though I knew God was with me, following the soul.

~ 7 ~

Checking Things Out

As soon as I stepped into my apartment, Deuce hemmed me in against the wall and patted me down.

Lance came over and hit me in the head and said, "Well, you ain't hurt."

"I know, right?" Deuce added. "Where's your cell phone?"

"It's in the car."

I was exhausted; obviously they had been worried about me. With everything I had gone through with the police and the sting and all I hadn't really had time to give them much thought.

"I'm alright," I said to the both of them as I headed toward the kitchen.

"It's five in the morning, Perry," Deuce said to me. "Don't get an attitude with me because we were concerned about where you had been. We've been blowing up your phone and the least you could have done was call us back. You left out of here with Mario and he was high. We didn't know where to go to find you or if you were lying up dead somewhere. It just is irresponsible for you to not touch base with us."

"Irresponsible? Come on, man," I said.

Lance cut in, "Wait, hold up, Perry, you are always the one

saying we are our brother's keeper and stuff and here you are blowing it off like it's no big deal. He's right; you got an attitude because we cared. What's up with that?"

"What's up with that is that—shoot, Lance. It's just that my cell's battery was dead and I was tied up."

"Tied up with what? Give us an explanation."

I knew if I told the two of them what really happened they would never let me live it down. They told me to leave Mario alone and I just had to try and help him out.

"I'm tired y'all . . . I'm tired. Can we talk about this tomorrow?"

"Mmm-mmm." Deuce stood in front of me, blocking me from being able to go into my space.

It was what it was; I might as well come clean and let them know what happened. I wasn't irresponsible. It's just that with everything I had gotten myself into, the last thing I needed was tension in the house.

"Alright, let's sit down and talk," I said to the both of them, pointing toward the couches. It took them no time to oblige me. Lance put his hands underneath his chin and sat on the edge of his seat waiting for me to say something. Deuce crossed his arms, like whatever I was going to say wasn't going to justify why I had not contacted them.

"Alright, you want to know. Here it is. Mario said he needed a ride because he didn't have his car anymore. He asked me to take him someplace where he could get clean."

Lance said, "Yeah, we wondered that too."

"Habit, I guess. But it got me into a lot of trouble."

"What do you mean?" Deuce said, unfolding his arms like he was concerned. "Man, what did that boy go and get you into?"

"I thought I was taking him to a halfway house to get clean and he's got me going to deliver drugs."

"And you did it?" Deuce said.

"NO, I didn't even know what he was doing."

"And then what happened?"

"Police raided the car. I was waiting on him to come back out. He said that he went in to go get some clothes or some junk, and I got manhandled. They had been checking him out for a while so they sort of believed my story when I told them. I had to be a front for them to catch him."

"Dang, boy. So where's Mario now?" Lance said.

"He's in jail."

"That's just unbelievable." He stood up and went to the window. "He had everything going for him. He was a senior at Tech and was betting on games. I mean he was one of the tightest quarterbacks around, he certainly could have played in the NFL and like now, it's all gone. Perry you can't be fooling with him no more," Lance said, "because you been done joined him."

"Yeah, I know."

"So did they file any charges?"

"Not against me, but I am still considered a person of interest in the case so I need to keep my nose clean, so I'm sorry I didn't call any of you guys. I was worn out. I feel bad for having to rat him out."

"Man, please," Deuce said. "You know Mario used to be my boy, but mmm-mmm. When it comes to choosing between you and him, and he's pulling you down the wrong road, dude, you got to cut that rope loose, let him fall where he falls. I just don't know why we can't be responsible for our own actions."

I actually couldn't believe I was hearing Deuce sound so positive. Any mom would be proud to hear her son talk that way. He was talking about his goals and dreams and not messing that up. Had Lance and I gotten to Deuce?

March was right around the corner. Two more months before our freshman year was over and maybe we would be okay after all. Still feeling compassionate for Mario, I said to them, "Hey, maybe we can pray for him."

"Yeah, cause I can't even imagine what jail is like," Lance admitted.

"Well, I was in handcuffs tonight and it wasn't no picnic."

"Next time you are ever in a jam like that think about us, call us or something. We've got to never leave out of here without our phones fully charged," Deuce said. "There's so much that we can get into and we have to look out for one another. We already lost one roommate. I just don't want to lose either one of you guys."

I nodded. Lance went over and slapped his hand.

I prayed, "Father, we come to You right now, lifting up Mario and everything going on with him. He's really at a place where he needs You, Lord. He's been selling and using and his mind is messed up. He's hanging with the wrong crowd and his life is really in danger. The cops want to squeeze on him and go after bigger fish. I don't even know, now I'm tied up into all of this mess. I just put it all up to You and ask You to work it out. Give us discernment to show the way in which we should go. We know You can fix what is broken, and right now Mario needs You and I need You too. Thank You for my roommates who care. Thank You for allowing me to get out of my troubles tonight Lord. I just love, praise You and I thank You. In Jesus' name, amen."

Lance said, "Amen."

Deuce said, "Amen."

Two or more were gathered and we certainly needed God to hear our prayer. As I headed off to bed I had faith that God would keep His word and be there for our fallen friend.

* * *

I couldn't believe spring was here. Winter had been such a harsh one, with the snow and the bitter cold. To see the flowers bloom was a breath of fresh air. All of my stuff in the closet were my winter clothes. My parents had hooked me up with a little allowance on a credit card, and since I couldn't fit into any of my clothes from last spring, even though I dreaded it, I had to head over to Atlantic Station to shop at Old Navy. I needed this to be easy and painless. Go in, grab a couple pair of jeans, shorts, some short-sleeve shirts, socks; maybe a new outfit to throw on at night and be done in twenty minutes—but they had all these new cuts. Low waist, boot cut; my mom used to shop for my stuff, throw it on the bed and be done; though I used to rag her about some of my outfits she had me pretty peppy. But now I had to be the big boy, go in the store and check things out. And it took me a while; I had a girl I had to represent. So I headed to an empty changing room to try on some of the latest threads. I used to be a 36, now I was a 38 in the waist—so I figured I would dash out and get the jeans in the right size and nobody would notice and I would be right back. Then I heard a female voice say, "Perry, is that you?"

And it wasn't Savoy. I was half-naked and I knew the luring tone she was using was letting me know that she was checking out my abs. I turned, dropping my hands to pull up my pants. It was Anna, the girl I had saved last summer after the rape—the one the cops mistakenly thought I molested. The one who finally came to and cleared me. She had been so beat up and bruised before that I didn't remember her being so beautiful. Her blond hair was wavy and down her back, bouncing and inviting like waves in a pool. She wore a miniskirt and she had the best curves I had ever seen. When she smiled at me it was so pure and innocent like all the pain and hurt she had gone through had been washed away. It wasn't like she was an angel, but she had a certain presence and peace about her that made me take notice.

"I'm working here. Can I help you with something?" she said, getting me back to reality.

"Umm, yeah, yeah. I need a bigger size in this."

When she stepped behind me to look at the tag I pulled away and said, "Oh, I need a thirty-eight."

"Oh, okay, I didn't think you knew what size you needed. You know I don't mind looking, but you still have that girlfriend, right?"

I couldn't remember at that moment if that was a good thing or a bad thing, but I did own up to the fact that I was already tied. She came back and brought me a couple of different things. Like my sister hooking me up or something. We just laughed and as I tried on a couple of things she was sharing that she wished that she had someone that loved God and was in school—smart, maybe athletic.

"Somebody just like you, Perry," she said, "but not you, of course, because you already have a girlfriend and I definitely wouldn't want a man with a girlfriend and that would just be horrible to get in and mess up your relationship and start on a bad foot and . . ."

"Okay, okay. I got it," I said to her. Why girls always rambled on and on was something I couldn't exactly figure out. "Well you said you wanted someone that loved God, and relationships are a lot of work, and let me tell you just keep praying about it. It'll work out."

"Alright. Well, not like you're going to need it to go out or anything, but here's my number the next time you have to go shopping you know; you can let me know and I'll hook you up."

"Yeah, it's no problem for me to take your number. I mean we're cool together, you alright from all of that?"

"Yeah, I'm good. Still have a few nightmares here and there but that guy is serving time for what he did to me."

"Oh snap really, they had the trial and everything?"

"Nope! That's why they didn't have to call you. He pleaded and it's over. He gets a shorter sentence but at last he's thinking about he took advantage."

"Cool."

The next day I was at home making some tuna fish to get me some energy to work out, and Lance came in and grabbed my sandwich out of my hand after I had already taken a bite and said, "See, if I had a girlfriend I would have someone who would make this for me. You've got to hook me up with somebody. I am tired of being lonely. I've put the nasty magazines down. I'm not into porn. I just want a girl to rub on, hold her hand, something. You won't let me have Savoy, so, shucks. I guess you gon' have to be my girl." He puckered up as he tried to kiss me.

"Boy, get back!" I said, retreating to the other side of the kitchen. But then I started thinking, *Hmm-mmm, Anna and Lance.*

The things she said she wanted he basically had; I knew he was a jerk, but what guy isn't? And though I hated to admit it I loved the boy to pieces now.

"Maybe I could hook you up."

"What, for real, Savoy got a track girlfriend?"

"Why all the black girls got to run track and what makes you think that I don't know any white girls? Heck, I go to Georgia Tech, they're all over here."

"Yeah, but you ain't talking to nobody new. Savoy would have your head."

"Well, let's just say regardless of what she looks like you would think she's hot. Would you go out with her?"

"You setting me up?"

"Mmmm, yeah, I guess I can check it out." I knew he wouldn't be disappointed. I just had to somehow get Anna excited about him. Maybe God was using me to make a connection. It was no harm in trying. If it didn't work out, they could at least be friends. From being a student, then a believer and a football player, now I was a matchmaker. I was a hard working brother.

It was seven AM on Saturday when my phone rang; I jumped up in a hurry, hoping nothing was wrong,

"HELLO, hello?"

"Hey, little brother," my sister said, sounding upset.

"Hey, girl. What's going on with you? Payton, what's going on girl? You don't sound alright."

"Cheerleading tryouts are today and I'm just stressed."

"Whatever, you know all them tricks and those flips—I mean you're the bomb. You have nothing to worry about."

"We have a new cheerleading sponsor and he is raising the bar. We are going to start doing competitions and he's out to beat Kentucky. A former Kentucky cheerleader. I don't know, truth be told I just guess I miss Grandma."

"I know, you know she's looking down on you. She's up there able to do a higher flip than you."

"Boy, you so silly," she finally said, laughing. "Yeah, I'll be alright and if I don't make it God has got something else for me right?"

I didn't know if that was a trick question, like if I said *Yeah, right* she would come back with, *See, I told you I wouldn't make it*, but if I said *You're going to make it* then she would say, *Well what if I don't make it? Would He have anything else for me?* My sister was so dramatic. I just blurted out, "I don't have anything to do today, how about I come up there?"

"What, you would do that?"

"Yeah, you supported me when we had a game and y'all had time off, I'll come up there if you want me to."

"What's Laurel's brother up there into?"

"Lance? Let me see if he can ride. Laurel's trying out again too."

"That's a good idea. Tryouts are at ten though, so you need to get up and get going."

"Bye girl."

An hour later Lance and I were on the road. He fussed, "I can't believe you dragged me out of bed so I could watch her try out for cheerleading. This is a joke right? Is this where the girl lives that you are introducing me to? I'm not coming all the way up here to see my sister; she's already a cheerleader, of course she's going to make the squad."

"Well, Payton told me it's not automatic. Something about a new coach."

"Whatever, man. You know your sister is over the top."

"I hear you, man."

"Isn't it interesting how they used to be roommates and cheer together and now we hooked up?" Lance asked me all out of the blue.

Us guys didn't really know how to express our feelings, we didn't wear them on our sleeve or anything. It wasn't easy for us to just be transparent, but I think he was trying to say that he really appreciated our growing bond and I did want to look deeper, care about my boys a little more, so I said, "You ain't half bad, Shadrach. Even though I still remember you trying to take my girl when I first met you."

"Aw, come on now, Perry. You had dissed her. You need to be thanking me."

"Thanking you, what?"

"Come on, check this out. If I hadn't of gotten with her, you wouldn't have gotten jealous and wanted her back, right?"

"Boy please, I had wanted her back way before she lost her mind thinking you had something on the ball."

We just laughed. It was really good just hanging out with him. We knew the only way to really have our relationship grow was to keep God in the center of it to make sure that we were keeping each other accountable.

Later, as we sat there watching our sisters try out and their names had been called again as Georgia cheerleaders, we didn't waste time giving them the flowers we picked up from the local Kroger grocery store and getting back on the road.

"I'm serious man, you gon' hook me up with a girl—obviously she's a believer. You think she's alright? I want to meet her."

"I don't know. I've been rethinking it all."

"See, see. Perry, what, dang!"

"I mean she's been through a lot, this chick. She's been through a lot. I'm not going to put her business out there and stuff, but I just don't know if you're ready."

"I mean, I know I'm in a different place. I was a knucklehead for quite some time, but finally being able to experience the position of starting quarterback humbled me. Getting out there and having the crowd boo. I learned that you may want some things but you really better be ready for them, and I do want a female in my life, if she's cool. I'm ready to do the right thing."

When we stopped off for gas and he went to go use the john I called up Savoy.

"Hey babe, you got plans tonight?"

"Hey babe, I miss you. I'm definitely excited to see you."

"I got a favor though."

"Uh oh, what is it?"

"That whole double date thing? You hated it, I know, but I'm trying to hook Lance up."

"With who? I ain't got no girls he'll like."

"I don't know if you remember that girl that I met when I was at Hilton Head?"

"Oh Blondie!"

"Her name's Anna."

"Yeah, Blondie. I know her, what? She was looking at you."

"So, Lance was looking at you."

"Maybe all four of us will be down for doing the same thing—you down for us hooking up?"

"As long as I don't have to be her girlfriend it will be cool."

"You ain't gon' be rude or nothing are you?"

"Perry, me rude?"

I gave her Anna's number and she told me she would coordinate the details and call me back if Anna couldn't do it. Otherwise, Lance and I would head straight over to Max & Irvinn's Pub where they had arcade games and good food.

"I'ma treat you, man," I said as we walked into the place.

"Good, cause you know my folks still got me on limited income," Lance teased.

"So, you really want to meet that girl? You gon' do the right thing?" I asked him as I looked around for Savoy.

"Yeah, when can we do it? Next week?"

"How about now?" I smiled as I turned his head over to Savoy. She waved at the two of us and motioned for us to come over.

"Well, I know that ain't her, that's your girl."

And then Anna stood right beside her wearing a cute black dress, not outshining my girl, but both of them were fly, and the dudes all up in the place were checking the two of them out. Lance hit me in the back.

"Alright, alright. I see what you doing. Let's go."

I knew he liked her. After we had dinner Savoy and I left to go play games and leave the two of them to talk. I knew the way they were staring at each other there was some kind of connection, but I had done my part. It was time for them to see if they could make a go of it. How would they know unless they had some alone time to be able to thoroughly start checking things out?

~ 8 ~

Getting into Danger

"Son, I need to talk to you right now," my dad said with a stern face as he stepped on my doorstep unannounced.

"Hey Dad, sure. Yeah, come in," I said, wondering what in the heck I had done now. I had gotten a few Cs on some papers, which was very unlike me, but I didn't think Tech was in the business of sending quiz grades home. Yeah I had spent a little money on the card, but it was nowhere near maxed out. I had even gone to support my sister and I got right back up and went back to school, so something was up. I hope he didn't come up here to say I was rude or something. What was this visit all about?

"I'm not trying to come in, son, you need to get your wallet, keys, personals, whatever and come on out. We need to take a ride. Hey guys!" my dad said to Lance and Deuce. He waited outside while I grabbed my things.

My boy Deuce said, "Ooh, somebody's in trouble."

"What did you do?" Lance asked.

"My dad's standards are so high he makes what Jesus requires look like bad parenting, you know what I'm saying," I chuckled.

"You know I understand—every other night my dad's calling me asking me have I done this or that," said Lance.

"Just take it like a man and move on, at least you've got a father that cares," Deuce said. "You too Lance. I haven't seen mine in ages. I would say stay out of trouble, but since you are going to be with pops . . . you straight."

"He, he!" I said to Deuce.

When I met my dad outside, he said, "Son, I don't need your smack, I need to get on back to Augusta."

"Alright Dad, what do you want to do, walk somewhere to talk?" All of a sudden he back-handed me on the back of my head.

"Ouch, what was that for?"

"Get in the car, boy."

He unlocked the sports car, and I couldn't even appreciate how fly it was because obviously he was tip.

"What have you been thinking, Perry? You go from hanging with one suspect character to hanging with another. I can't believe how gullible you are sometimes."

All of a sudden I felt like someone had punched me in the chest. Had the feds called my dad?

He confirmed my worst fear by saying, "I got a call from the Drug Enforcement Agency informing me that they need your cooperation."

"Dad, I told them I would cooperate in any way they needed me to," I said, almost pouting. It was none of his business; I was a grown man now. I had to take care of my own problems. Yeah, I had made a mess and now I was ready to clean it up.

"Well, let me just say right now, with as much as you have on the ball, to get caught up in some federal scam! They want you to go to that jail and talk to Mario, to tell him to confess about some other bigger ring."

"Dad, I can't make him do or say nothing!"

"Well, if he can make you say and do stuff and land you in this situation, then you need to find out how to be persuasive and get him to do what's in your best interest and his. Son, you used to be a leader and now all this following stuff, all this *I don't want to get my hands dirty*, it's too late for that. Your hands got mud on 'em and I hope it ain't sat in there so long it won't come off. I can't believe you ain't call me when you had to talk to the cops. That mess is illegal, we could have had them right then and there. Thankfully you cleared yourself on the tape but we don't know what some of this leaked. And if what they're asking is for you to persuade that guy to talk so he can get out of jail, then you need to be the very first one up there tomorrow morning. Skip whatever class, whatever test, whatever Coach wants you to do and get your butt down there to the federal penitentiary. They're already waiting on you to be there at eight."

I sighed.

The next morning, I couldn't believe I was walking with the same crazy agent that had opened his mouth and ratted on me to my pops in the first place. Now he wanted my help, but he'd gone behind my back and made this even more of an issue.

"Why couldn't you have just asked me?" I said to him as we walked through the triple set of steel doors.

"Son, protocol says because you aren't twenty-one there are certain things we have to do. You might not like that, I can understand that, but this is my job and I'm not here to make friends. Now you have a job to do, you need to convince your boy to talk to us."

"Just how do you expect me to do that, Mr. Right-by-the-Book?" I asked.

"I don't know and I don't really care, but I know you're smart and a creative boy. You'll figure something out." Then he turned around and slammed the door, leaving me in a room alone. Then I heard through an intercom that Mario would be in in just a second, feel free to sit, stand, and do whatever I liked. I was so angry to be here in the first place that I didn't really take in the eeriness of the whole place. I know most of the men that are incarcerated are black, and it just made my skin feel like a spider was crawling all over it at the thought of feeling trapped, unable to come and go as I pleased, only able to eat when someone says.

Alright Lord, I know you get tired of me time after time coming to You asking You for help but I need You, give me the words to say.

"I can't believe they brought me in here to see you," Mario said quickly, then he banged on the door that they had just brought him through and said, "Let me out now. I don't want to see this person. Let me out."

"Come on man, Mario. Can you just hear me out?"

"What, what you got to say to me? You the one who got me in this mess."

"Hold on, partner. It's because of you that you're in here and you're having to deal with this."

"You don't know what it's like in here."

"So, you need to work with the feds to get out."

"And then what, be dead? I don't think so. I'll just deal with the thugs looking at me from every direction, looking at me like I'm their new meat."

"Mario, you really have got a lot on the ball, you're so tough, man. The only reason you're doing all of this is because you were pressured into this in the first place. Turn the heat back on those crooks. They're selling dope back to our community, messing up our race, messing up our future, messing up America."

"Oh, so what, you signed up for the army now?"

"I'm just saying don't let them let you take the fall, while they continue to sabotage the world, pushing us stuff. Don't do it."

For about five minutes we just looked at each other.

"I know it won't be easy cooperating, but just think about it, man," I said finally, realizing that he had to want this for him. "I'll be here for you, dude. I care about you a lot."

I got up, knocked on the other door and got out.

Five days had gone by and the feds had called me every single one of them.

"Your boy isn't cooperating. You must not have said the right things."

Now, they heard everything I said, I did all I could, but yet I was the one to blame because Mario was taking the heat, wanting to stay in prison and take the fall. I kept praying—I even fasted, which was something I hadn't done in a long time. Legally they didn't have anything on me, they couldn't charge me, but ethically it could really screw me up if I was tied to all of that. When the phone rang and the prison's phone number came up, I was so uneasy. I was hoping that it wasn't them wanting me to come back up there and talk to him again. I had given it all I could and I was so shocked to hear Mario's voice.

"Man, it's me. I've been thinking about what you said, dude, and they are about to let me out of here. I told them all I know and he's going down."

"You need to stop by the crib a little later. We need to celebrate."

"I got to go gather my things and then they going to move me. Perry, you there?"

"Yeah, I'm here. I'm just shocked; it's been a couple of days and I didn't think you gave a crap about what I had told you."

"Yeah, I heard you. I heard you. I messed up a lot of things at school and I know the fans think I'm crazy, but I got talent. I can play in the USFL, I can play in Canada. Give me a chance I can play on someone's practice squad and play in the Super Bowl one day. The sky's the limit, when I clear myself of all of this I can then be back on track."

"That's what I'm talking about Mario, yeah."

"Plus, I've been clean. I've been in jail for these two weeks. I'm able to think. Those drugs can mess a dude up, you know?"

"Yeah, man, I know."

"You don't know, boy, you ain't never smoked nothing."

"I'm just saying I ain't got to smoke it to know what it do to folks. So you about to get out, cool. I'ma see you later, right?"

"Yeah man, yeah."

"Mario, man . . . ummm, I didn't want to say it overly sensitive like a girl or whatever . . ." I was proud of him, I just didn't know how to come out and let him know it.

"I got you man, I got you."

"Yeah man, you feeling me? Cool." As I hung up the phone I didn't realize that I had two eavesdroppers listening to my every word.

"Dang, can a brother have a conversation without everyone in the whole world trying to hear him?"

"Alright, I know he's getting out of jail, but I know you not about to go and hang out with him," Deuce said. "That's just crazy, man."

"Yeah, man, that's just like asking for trouble all over again. What you doing opening the door to trouble?"

"He's clean, okay? He's getting out of jail."

"Yeah, okay. He gon' say whatever he got to say to get you back over there. He knows you got a couple of dollars from your daddy, he knows you'll feel some sort of obligation from him blaming you for all his mess, but man, please don't fool with him," Deuce commented.

I just sat down on the couch and scratched my head. They

had a point, but I had to believe that Mario learned a great lesson and I was smarter now. I could believe and trust everything he said.

"He's my boy, okay? I'm not trying to be disloyal to people, okay. How you treat people comes back on you, plus the word says we're supposed to be our brother's keeper."

"Yeah, and doesn't it say that we're supposed to flee from fornication and guilt and a bunch of other reasons why you should not be hanging out with Mario?" Lance pointed out.

"Right, right," Deuce said.

"I hear y'all and I appreciate you."

Deuce came over and shook me. "Listen, get it through your brain that hanging with him will be real stupid. Mario is slick, Perry. I know you think you know a lot and I'm glad you speaking the word and what Jesus said and all that. I know I'm trying to grow in my word too, but some folks you just got to let loose. You let him know cooperating was the best thing for him and now what, you gon' give him a chance to screw you again?"

"Get off me!" I said, brushing his hand off my shoulder.

"Alright, fine. Do what you want to, but if you end up in jail for real, messing with this dude again, don't come calling me. I'm telling you right here and now that he is crazy. I was the one who went there with him, remember? I was the one saying give him a chance. Let him do this and do that. Lance was the one that knew he was foul. I got burned once by him. It ain't goin' be no more. You, it's been what, three or four times? Come on, Perry, don't be stupid."

I walked into my room and slammed the door. Oh, I had heard what they said and it had made so much sense.

My phone rang later on that night and when I saw that it was Mario, I didn't pick it up. Shoot, he wasn't going to get me into something else.

The next day Mario called me seven times. I ignored all of

his calls but then when I was in class and flipped it open because I forgot to turn it off, he just started screaming. "I thought you was my boy? I thought you cared about me. You get me out here and then you ain't nowhere out here to help."

"Help you with what, Mario? You just said you out, what you need me for?"

"Trying to move some of my stuff to storage."

"You got protection for that."

"We talked about it man, I don't need none."

"What?!"

"They told me to take a few days to think about it, but I don't need none. Ain't nobody messing with me. They don't even know I'm messing with them like that, but it ain't like I got somebody to hang out with that's worth something. You talk about God. You talk about me living my life the right way and then when I need you to be there for me, to hang out and stuff, show me where I'm supposed to go, you just kick me to the curb? You a trip man, I ain't trying to get you in no trouble. I'm trying to get at you to help me stay out of it. Whatever though, I should have known you ain't no good."

Was he right?

All through the rest of my class I couldn't concentrate. Mario's accusations were weighing heavily on my mind. How could I convince him of doing the right things if I slipped from him completely? In the Bible, Jesus went into the bars when the disciples had messed up, to win souls for Him. If I was going to be ready to stand up for God I was going to have to be ready for anything that came. If Jesus could be crucified and get up and rise from the dead, certainly He was protecting me, and I really felt a strong calling that He wanted me to help. I knew where Mario stayed—he had an apartment right off of campus. I went over there and he was gathering his stuff.

"I thought you didn't need no protection?" I joked, knocking on the frame of the open door.

"I don't need them to know exactly where I'm staying, you know what I'm saying. I got to be a little smart about this thang. Come in dog, dang. I'm surprised to see you."

"I know, I know. I've been MIA, I wasn't just trying to just leave you out there though, man. I just. I don't know."

"You wanted to make sure I didn't pull you down, get you into any more trouble. I realize I let you down and that I had hung you out there to dry. I think we even now, cool?"

We slapped hands and had a cool embrace. We were taking boxes out of the apartment to his car, when all of a sudden, he yelled, "Get down man, get down! They rolling up on the house."

"What, what are you talking about man?" As soon as I turned around he hit me in the back and pushed me to the ground and shots rang out. It was madness.

"Dang man, they know. Stay down man, stay down." He inched his way over to the trunk and pulled out a nine millimeter.

"Man, where'd you get that gun?"

"Man, I ain't stupid. I didn't need the feds to protect me, but I was going to have protection. Don't get up Perry, don't get up."

I couldn't believe this. As soon as I was trying to do the right thing trouble found me. I thought they had left, then five jokers got out of the car—but when Mario started shooting they didn't come close to us.

"T-Money, get back man. You don't want to lose your life, man."

"You don't want to lose yours either. You told 'em about

me and they trying to find me. They got my girl pent up and she's eight months pregnant. They said if I don't turn myself in they are going to lock her up on some bogus charge all because of stuff you told them."

"Whatever, man. It ain't even like that."

"Oh, so you didn't keep your mouth shut?"

Some more shots rang out. Mario ducked.

"Man, we got to run."

"Ha, where man? Bullets are faster than human legs. Even your million dollar ones alright? Now you just stay down."

Over the last few months there had been many times when it felt like my life was flashing before me: when I had drank way too much alcohol and it felt like my heart was about to bust, when J. Bo and his boys beat me up, and when I got another beating at Hilton Head. But it was weird—just as I thought, *Lord you need to protect me,* I felt like a big igloo covered my entire body, and though I could hear more gunfire, I felt safe. I couldn't explain why and I didn't know how I was going to get out of it, but even if safe meant leaving this world and being with God it would be a place where I found peace. It was something about doing the right thing, not fleeing from trying to help somebody out of their darkness. It was like God was going to show me light.

"You going to Hell tonight," the dude named T-Money said to Mario.

"Yeah, whatever. It ain't real."

"I guess you'll never know. I'm sorry, God," Mario said as he shot right in between T-Money's eyeballs. He fell to the floor. His boys got in their car and jetted away.

"It's over man, it's over."

"We've got to go see if he's alright."

"He ain't moving, man. I had to kill him or he was going to kill me."

T-Money had said he didn't believe in God. With all of the

blood on his hands from his past sins I knew I wasn't going to see him in Heaven. Though I didn't physically cry, inside I felt worse than the slaves I read about in *Roots*. Another black soul wasted—gone. As soon as I walked over to T-Money's body Mario called out, "They're coming back, they're coming back!"

This was unreal, like it was out of a daggone movie. I had no gun, I had no knife, I didn't even have a stick to try and defend myself with, and a part of me didn't want to fight.

"Run, boy," he said.

As shots exploded in the air I knew I had to do something to stop getting into danger.

~ 9 ~

Calming My Heart

"Wait, no. Stop man. Don't shoot at us," one of the rugged, scared voices shouted out from the car. I knew bullets had gone past me, but now that I had thought about it, it had all come from one particular direction; Mario had been the only one shooting. Yeah, the guys had come back. It was only natural for Mario to think that they were coming back to attack—after all, the leader of their crew was down. They took their bandanas off their heads and were waving them out of the window.

Mario kept shooting. It was like he couldn't hear what they were saying or he couldn't believe it, or was just so confused and changed by the fact that he had taken a man's life that he wasn't even responsive. Finally the gun was out of bullets and I stood up and said, "No more, Mario. No more, man."

"Perry, move out of my way."

The guys in the car stood up as well.

"They don't want to hurt you, man. Give me the gun, Mario."

When he just stood still, frozen like an ice block, I yanked the empty steel weapon from his shaking hands.

"Y'all want to talk, what?"

I turned around and said to them, "It's cool, it's clear."

"Don't get out of that car," Mario yelled, coming out of his trance.

"Mario, let's just talk to them, man."

"Perry, you don't understand. These guys do one thing and . . ."

"We just want to tell you we wanted to stay with you and talk to the cops; we were forced into this life too. He had a lot over us."

All four of them climbed out of T-Money's bullet-ridden car with their hands up.

The thick guy out first said, "Look, I'm Roscoe. We want to let the cops know that he ran up on you. Squash all of this; it's time for everyone to move on, alright?"

When I was little my mom always used to make me watch *The Wiz.* I not only had to see it on TV tons of times because my sister liked the movie, but every time it came to a theater in Atlanta we drove down to watch the play. I even played the scarecrow in middle school and I remember the ending: when the wicked witch was dead, all of the helpers were overjoyed. Such seemed like the case here. Maybe with T-Money gone it would be one neighborhood that could now survive. I guess other people had heard all of the confusion cause it didn't take long for the police to come, and it felt like déjà vu when I had to have my hands up in the air once again. But when we saw a familiar face because the feds had been called based on the address that came up in the computer system, it was good to know that the law was real receptive to finding out the truth. Those guys kept their word, and after we went downtown and gave full statements, we were free to go.

"Skky, I know it didn't seem like it was worth it, but because you stuck by my man a lot of people are going to be able to sleep a lot better tonight," the agent said. "The other guy's dead. I'm not here to judge anybody, but when you're cut from the devil's cloth, on earth is not a place where you need to be." He threw out a folder and flipped through T-Money's rap sheet, listing page after page of juvenile and adult crimes. His sheet was longer than a football field. "You think he needed to stay around? It was just he was so good at being a bully that nobody wanted to stand up to him, nobody wanted to admit what he was doing to the community. For you to get Mario to stand up, because Mario felt like he wasn't standing alone with your support, is heroic. We don't have an award or a medal and all that to give you, but I just want to say to you, son, I always heard you were a guy with character and your father certainly gave you his praises. Now I'm seeing it for myself, because we've been tailing the both of you guys."

I didn't want any accolades from him, though I wasn't disrespectful. This was still a lot to deal with—I had watched a guy die. The good thing though is that all of those under his command were now free, and I made it my own personal mission to make sure that I witnessed to each and every one of them. I didn't want them to have any idle time to think, *Oh, I can be the next king of the projects* and pick up right where T-Money left off. It really did my soul good to know that in the midst of the madness I was seeing that God had a purpose for me. I wasn't overly optimistic, thinking I would be able to have every one of those guys falling on their knees in repentance, but knew that I was going to give it my all to tell them about the One that loved them so much.

"Y'all, I just don't want to go anywhere for spring break. It's been a long semester and I still have to make it through exams. I really need to study. I have big man problems, you know what I'm saying?"

"Then the only way to rid yourself of all that stress is to come with me down to Florida," Saxon said. "Don't worry, my sister ain't goin' to get mad if you go with me. She'll think we're babysitting each other."

I looked at Deuce to help me out. I mean it wasn't like I wanted to tell Saxon that I wouldn't be there for him. He had recuperated nicely and had really been doing well, with a full recovery leading up to Spring ball, and the last thing I wanted to do was let him down. But Deuce wasn't helping me out. He folded his arms like *Yep, so what you goin' to tell him cause I want to go to the beach.*

"Aw, boy, you ain't right, I thought you wanted to chill. I went last year to Florida on spring break and it was wild, but it wasn't that relaxing."

"Yeah, but you was in high school then, we college boys. We can have all the honeys and chill at our spot—my parents got a nice piece of timeshare right on the beach."

Lance had already said that he was going to Ft. Lauderdale with some of the other teammates and I was really looking forward to having the place all to myself, but clearly the two of them weren't letting up until I agreed to go. Like the softy I tried not to be, I nodded. Saxon tackled me. "That's my boy, that's my boy. Yeah!"

It was interesting to see how a few months could change a person's heart. He had had much hatred for me early on, but I had prayed for God to soften his heart in regards to him understanding that I just didn't leave him out there when the dude attacked him. And in some way God just did His thing, and now that I had that friendship again my new goal was to make sure Saxon was saved. Maybe me going with Saxon to Florida wasn't such a bad idea after all.

The next day I took my girl out on a much needed date. Talk about relaxing, it was good to just sit in a movie theater, sleep holding her hand, knowing that we were all good. Expectations and pressure that were usually affiliated with us spending time together weren't there. She was happy to be there with me and I really appreciated that, which made me more into her. No expectations, just quality time spent. When we walked out of the movie theater we had ice cream and she brought up the Florida trip.

"So, you're going to behave yourself right?"

"Hey baby, if you don't want me to go just say the word." Knowing that I really didn't want to go anyway.

"No, Saxon's excited and my parents are glad you're going too."

"Why don't you come?"

"Yeah right, a sister/girlfriend hanging out on a boys' trip. No, it's the boys' time. I'm just happy the two of you guys aren't killing each other anymore."

"Yeah, what's up with that? You've been trying to defuse stuff between us lately?"

"No, not really, he's just changed. I think's it's the God thing," she said. "I love you and I trust you," she said, leaning in and giving me the sweetest kiss, tasting like berries or something.

"I miss those lips," I said, getting another one as I pulled her to me. There was nothing more relaxing than spending time with her. "So how wild do you think your brother is going to be on this trip?" I came out and asked her.

"Well, put it this way—my parents and I are really looking for you to keep him in check."

"Oh, you talking babysitting for real, for real?"

"Well, like I said, it'll be twofold because I know the word my man has, and I'm sure that girls are going to be trying . . ."

"Oh hush and come here." I pulled her close to me again. Maybe it was the ice cream I tasted but from her lips it was much more delicious than the one in my waffle cone. "So what you gon' do?"

"It's track season, I got to stay here with the girls and train. No spring break for me, but I won't be too mad if you cut yours short. Coach is going to give us one day off."

"Yeah, maybe we can do something."

The ride down to Ft. Lauderdale was a piece of cake. I had been there before, I knew the route, even though I didn't know the exact place we were staying. Saxon stopped every few miles for some beer. He must have had a fake ID to buy it. Though I wasn't cool wit' that method, I wasn't trying to argue. I only wanted to relax by the beach.

Thankfully, we got in before nightfall. The first place I headed was to see the waves rush in. Before I could get my feet wet, I heard someone call my name.

"Perry, hey it's me."

I knew the voice sounded familiar, not a white sweet voice, not a cool black one, but one in between. When I turned around I was shocked to see my cousin Pillar prancing up to me wearing the skinniest two-piece I had ever seen.

"Girl, you need to cover up. Dang!"

"How am I going get my groove on if I look like grandma? I had a hard year, transferring to a new place. I made a few friends."

All of a sudden I felt someone rubbing on my back, I looked around and it was Rain, my sister Payton's high school best friend. They were both at Spelman. When she started feeling in between my legs my heart was anything but calm. Trouble was, she looked so good that it felt so right. This little vacation that was supposed to be drama-free had just intensified.

My heart skipped a few beats, like her touch got to me or something. To be honest, Rain, who was much sexier than I remembered with her tall slender frame, was the first girl I ever had a thing for. She was at a slumber party with my sister. She was a ninth-grader and I was in the seventh grade. I walked in on her in the bathroom, and boy did I get a surprise. It was funny because even though she covered up it wasn't like she was quick to block me from seeing everything. I mean she was good, I just think if I had been a little older I would have had a chance. But now as I stood taller than her, finally with muscles that would impress her, maybe my chance was now.

"What, you not going to give me a hug?" she said, looking me up and down. I could tell as her tongue rolled that she wished she was doing more than looking at me. I had to bite my tongue. Though I was cool and collected I was anything but calm. I had a girl and I was excited about that, I was only here to help her brother show out. Trouble was not supposed to find me and temptation certainly wasn't supposed to know where I would be, but just like normal, both of them peeped me out. I gave her a hug and felt her breasts rub up against my chest; I couldn't figure out if she was trying to seduce me or if that was happening because the daggone bathing suit she had on looked like two strings.

"So you guys are going to come over and let us cook for you?" she said as she pulled away, still holding both of my hands. Saxon was so caught up in checking out my cousin that he wasn't even catching up on the vibes that were going on between me and Rain—which was cool because I certainly didn't need him making me feel worse than I already felt.

I went over to my cousin and said, "Girl, for real you need to put some clothes on."

"My dad is back in Arizona."

I looked at her like, *Are you kidding me?* Some of the offensive linemen from Tech were down there and Deuce had hooked up with them, so Saxon and I went to the condo where my cousin and Rain and a few other chicks from Spelman were staying. I liked Savoy, because she had a touch of class, but some of the girls she hung around with or even some of the girls that used to be at my old school weren't like these Spelman chicks. I mean they had it going on, sisters with . . . not arrogance, but confidence—were just attractive. The way they looked at me let me know that they were intrigued but they weren't throwing themselves on me. They knew they had it going on with or without me, but Rain, with her long legs and her hair blowing in the breeze, made me get up and chase after her when she dashed to the beach.

She turned around and said, "You can't catch me."

I loved looking at the view from behind, but if she was going to tease a brother what was I going to do but oblige? When I caught up to her we lost our footing and fell into the sand, with me on top of her looking down into her eyes.

She said to me, "I couldn't wait on you growing up. I didn't want to go to jail for robbing the cradle, but now you're a man, Perry Skky Jr. A fine man at that."

She leaned up and brushed my neck with her lips. It was soothing. I felt relaxed but then I rolled off of her.

"We can't. We can't!" I said out loud.

She rolled over on her side and looked at me. "You've probably been pressured every day to get with a girl and go all the way. I didn't mean to be forceful, I just had some old feelings and some new ones and you are hot. And if Payton heard me saying these words your sister would kill me."

"You're looking pretty good too. My sister doesn't run me, that's not the problem."

She kissed my lips. "What is? I don't want to know. Let's just enjoy each other. This is spring break—I know you're supposed to have flings. I know you're big man on campus—shoot, the boys at Morehouse even know who you are. I'll get mad points when they know we went to school together.

They wager if you're going to make it to the pros one day, but I know the true Perry Skky, the little guy who worked overtime to reach his dream. You didn't just arrive, and you had a dad that was on you. And you used to fall down on your knees and pray for God to make you better."

"You saw that?" I said, shocked to remember those days of riding the bench in the seventh grade. I was real frustrated that my body was developing slowly, unlike the other boys in my class.

"Yeah, I watched you a lot. Your sister would get on me all the time, but the guys in my grade were so fast. Of course I thought you were adorable and then the time you saw me bare in the bathroom." I couldn't even continue to look at her, I just turned away. "Wait, wait. Don't be bashful now I've really got something for you to see."

She took my hand and placed it on her chest. I closed my eyes, not needing to see a thing because what I was feeling was feeling real good, and then I felt my ears getting wet one at a time. People said this part of Florida was paradise and the way I was feeling was solidifying that fact. Yeah, I had a girl. Yeah, I was trying to honor God, but I had so much stress on me. Would it be all bad getting my groove on? I needed something settling or soothing for calming my heart.

~ 10 ~

Running from Love

"I'm on the pill," Rain said to me, looking deep into my eyes. "Let's go all the way Perry, make me feel good."

Our bodies had been grinding for the last few minutes even with lightning in the sky and darkness surrounding us. It just felt too good to pull away, but after that statement the thunder roared loud. It was like God was saying, "Boy don't be crazy, don't lose your mind. Get the heck up and tell her no."

It certainly wasn't like my loins wanted to hear all of that, but the spirit inside of me won the battle.

It wasn't about another pregnancy scare—she said we were covered. And it wasn't about me wanting to be true to my girl. I had already crossed the cheating line kissing on somebody else. It probably should have been some concern about the fear of a disease, but Rain was so ready to give it up to me it wasn't no telling who else she had laid up with. It was about God pulling at the strings of my soul. I just didn't want to hit it, I mean I did want to hit it, but it needed to be more. Not a physical attraction but a commitment, one that was holy, and that was something I certainly didn't have with Rain. Yeah, she was fly and certainly a turn-on with her body all gritty from the sand. As I tried hard to run from the love that mattered most, He just stood out and with the touch of nature He got me pretty good. The lightning bolt hit twenty feet away from us and that was too close.

"Alright, I hear ya," I said out loud.

"It'll be okay, we don't have to stop," she said, not getting it.

So I had to tell her, "Girl, it's not about the rain, it's about what that symbol of lightning means to me. It's a warning. I'm trying to do this thing with God and I'm trying to please Him and it is hard. It's real hard, but I can do it."

"Wow. I'm kind of impressed," she said. "I stopped walking that path when I first walked on my college campus. I had waited and waited to give myself to one guy and one guy only, only to find out that he had been messing around on me for years. I couldn't understand how a guy that was supposed to love me let me be so blind and let me fall when things didn't work out. Now, who cares about love? Who cares about promises, we're young, we're supposed to have fun. Everybody can't have what your sister has with that boy up there at Georgia."

"Yeah, you're right. She and Tad do have something special and it's not about anything else. A person's walk with God is special."

I was standing and reached down and pulled her up, and we started shaking off the sand.

And I said, "I better walk you back to your villa."

"You got class, Perry Skky Jr." She reached over and gave me a kiss on the cheek. "We'll cross paths again when the time is right. Your girl sure is lucky."

The rest of the way we walked back briskly in silence, while the thunder and lightning kept doing its dance and I thought about Savoy and how I let her down. She trusted me to come on a vacation and just be a chaperone for her brother but yet I couldn't even go a couple of days without yielding to temptation. I didn't think I could sleep without talking to her. I really didn't know if I needed her to forgive me because I didn't know if I could forgive myself, but I had to come clean. You know just like when you have to go to the john your stomach just won't sit still until it releases the waste.

"You were out awfully late," Deuce said as I came into the condo to get my cell phone. "Watch it now, you got lipstick on your cheek."

I just looked at him and he knew I was frustrated.

"Perry, it's hard for a brother. It's just hard."

"Yeah, well we got to do better."

"All of us gon' fit the stereotype all the time?"

"Naw, I know it's some men out there, real men that let God lead the way always. I just got to tap in too, it's already there I just got to do better. At least I care. Right?"

"Yeah man, at least you care. Your phone's been ringing. I think your girl's been calling."

"Yeah, I'ma call her up. Where's her brother?"

"Out with your cousin. He came back in here looking for some condoms, so umm . . ."

"Are you serious man? Where'd they go?"

Deuce threw his hands up in the air.

"Aw, seriously man. Where'd they go?"

"I don't know, but you can't make her cut him off."

"I know I can't make her, but he knows where I stand on all of that. But they just met."

"He told me he was in love!"

"And you believed that?"

"I don't know man, he ain't never told me that he was in love."

He had a point. I took my phone and headed back outside. I was shocked to see Saxon coming up the condo stairs.

"Where's my cousin, man?"

"I just want you to see that I haven't used these. I know Deuce opened his big mouth, but she's something special. I'ma see her tomorrow."

"Yeah she's something real special."

Since that was over, I called my girl.

"Hey, baby. I've been trying to get you," she said in the sweetest voice. I couldn't even respond. "So I guess that confirms what I've been thinking. You've been having a beach fling, huh?"

Still I couldn't say a word.

"I know God stopped you and I know you love me and I tried to tell you that girls would be coming after you left and right, but now maybe you'll see. You aren't untargetable."

"So how can I be a good boyfriend to you when I've got issues?"

"You think my eyes don't watch other guys?"

"Yeah, but you don't kiss all of them."

"Well, I don't want to know the details and I don't want to be with someone who is not satisfied with just me. But I don't think you're battling us. I think you're just battling the devil and you have to conquer him. Let him know that he can't be victorious. Think about it babe." And she hung up.

"Dang man, your girl is going to mess up the track meet, ain't she?" Marquez Jackson hit me in the arm at the track meet and said.

Savoy fell in the hurdles. I knew the girl had my heart because when she did it was like I was a parent or something, feeling really bad that she had made a major mistake for the team. The Tech girls were fighting to win the ACC, but their competition was the Miami Hurricane girls. And just when it seemed we have a chance to win, Savoy made a big mistake.

"Get up. Get up," I said in a small voice I hoped she could feel. Just as the trainer was headed her way she got up from the pavement and finished the race. "That's what I'm talking about."

"Whatever, man. Her time is going to be whack."

"Man, hush."

"Whatever, I got us to the National Championship game."

"It wasn't you alone," I said back to Marquez, letting him know that I didn't appreciate him talking about my girl.

"Don't get sensitive, you know how sports goes. Unless they have a heck of a time in the four-by-four relay she pretty much lost the meet for them."

They were getting ready to go into the last race and I saw Charlie and Jailyn stretching. Deuce and Jailyn had really been holding their relationship down. We hadn't talked about it a lot but she was working with a brother. She had him studying all the time. They trained together when they didn't have to train with their respective teams. She seemed like a cool girl and Charlie was still hot and crazy, leaving me messages here and there that I would erase without listening to. There was one other girl out there that I didn't know. She was faster than a bullet.

Then Marquez said, "That's my girl right there, DJ Wright."

"I didn't know you had a girlfriend."

"Whatever man, you know how we do, but that's her. She's gon' run in the Olympics. She's been saying how inconsistent that girlfriend of yours is, man. I know she don't want her to run the relay now."

Instantly I got up from the bleachers, jogged down the stairs, jumped over the fence and inconspicuously walked out onto the track.

DJ, with her hands on her hips, got up in Savoy's face and said, "You don't even need to be out here with us. Your piss-poor performance is bringing us down. The only place you need to run is away from us."

Jailyn and Savoy were still cool I thought, but when Jailyn

stood back with her arms crossed, not even defending her friend, I wondered what was up with that.

Charlie let her beef be known. "You quit on us in the last race. Why would we want you to run the relay knowing that something has got you upset and that you're not going to give your all."

Savoy put her hand over her lips and put her head down and when she looked up tears were flowing lightly like a stream. She just turned away from them and dashed toward the locker room.

I heard the coach call out, "Savoy, where are you going? The race is in a second. Come on back, Savoy."

But she didn't respond, she just headed to pack it in. Instead of jogging, I did a sprint. The guys were running their race and then it would be the girls; she didn't have a lot of time to be jiving around. I tried to catch up with her before she went into the locker room but I was unsuccessful, so I threw my hands in the air and said bump it. Sometimes you just had to do what you had to do and it was a good thing I went in to the locker room. The light tears I saw on the field paled compared to the sobbing she was doing as she pounded her fists on the lockers.

"Hey, hey," I said, putting my body in between the locker and her fists.

"Perry, please move. Please. I'm not in the mood, just leave me alone. I told you not to come to this meet anyway."

"Well, I had some time on my hands and I wanted to be out there for you."

"Well, you saw that I choked. Everything that coach told me about lifting up my leg, stay in my lane and concentrate, I couldn't even do. I messed up the meet and my teammates don't even want me to run with them, okay. And if I got out there I don't even know if my little old heart would be into it."

"I know girls can be ruthless at times with the things that they say. What you think, I don't have to deal with the same crap from the guys on the field, talking trash trying to psyche me out mentally. And remember you are talking to the guy who basically lost the season opener due to my piss-poor performance. Look at me girl, I understand."

She fell into my arms. "I was supposed to be so good, but ever since I ran into DJ, I don't know, I just haven't been able to step up my game."

"Competition is supposed to challenge you, being around the best is only supposed to make you better."

"Yeah, but . . ."

"No, no buts. You got a God that gave you mad skills, but that doesn't mean you're always going to be perfect. When I messed up in that first game I committed to the rest of the season that I would make up for it for my team. If track and field is what you care about then know that you know that you got it. Shake off the fear and do your thing."

"You really think I can?"

"The question is do you believe that you can?"

She nodded, headed out on the field, ran as lead anchor in the next race, and they won.

"We won, we won!" Savoy said as she came up to me. "Are we going to celebrate tonight, let's do something. Because of you, I turned it around and we won."

I appreciated that she was all excited; I was happy that I could step in and recharge her. But I wasn't feeling the whole get-together thing; I couldn't explain it. I didn't know where that was coming from. I wasn't sick. I didn't have no major test to study for or nothing like that.

I just said, "Naw, let's just take a rain check."

Her whole demeanor just deflated, her arms dropped, her smile vanished; she sighed.

"I don't know, I'm just not trying to go out and stuff," I said.

"Well, I can come over. We can watch a movie or something like that."

But there was no way that I could be like, *you know what, I just don't want to be around you tonight.* "Well, can we just get a bite to eat right now?" I said.

"No, Coach wants to talk to us and stuff. You want to wait forty-five minutes or an hour to eat?"

"Naw, I'm starving."

"What's going on Perry? I mean, is there something you're not saying? You got back last week and told me you had your lips on another girl."

"Naw, I don't know if I said *that*."

"What, are you denying it? she asked. I don't even know why I asked you to spend a Saturday night with me. You know what? Have it your way."

She turned around and stormed off. I wanted to call her back and say alright, let's do something, but there wasn't a need to fake the funk. I went home and just passed out on the couch. Both of my roommates were excited about the females in their lives. Things were working out between Lance and Anna, and Deuce had gotten with Jailyn since he didn't make it to the track meet. There was no reason why I couldn't have Savoy over with me, besides that us being in an apartment all by ourselves with a bed nearby might have provoked temptation, but I knew deep down that wasn't it. What was I distancing myself from? The Bible was on the coffee table in front of me. I had no desire to pick it up and read anything, but then Psalms 23 came to my memory. I said the last part out loud, "Surely goodness and mercy shall follow me all the days of my life." So where the heck are goodness and mercy at now? And when I laid my head back on the back of the couch, it felt like two angels sat on either side of me. I don't know if I was dreaming, tripping or thinking about some of the TV shows I had been watching about angels paying a visit to folks, but whatever it was that moment was real enough for me to see Goodness as a beautiful movie star type lady, and Mercy as some crazy comedian.

You called? said Mercy.

Of course he called, that's why we're here, Goodness uttered back to him.

My angels had style.

You've got to know that we're here all of the time, Perry.

My mouth wasn't moving but I thought, *Yeah, but you don't do a good job of it. You're supposed to be my angels but I get in more trouble . . .*

But aren't you still here, dude? Mercy said.

Well what's going on with you? I asked.

That's for you to figure out, Goodness said. *Just keep your heart pure. If you're not feeling it don't force it. You're doing the right thing.*

But I'm letting down my girl; I haven't even talked to my parents. I just don't feel like God can use me.

Because you want Him to, He will, and though Savoy is a jewel you guys are young, Goodness said.

Why am I so hot and cold with her?

Again, that's for you to find out. That book is right in front of you. It's a road map to life. Pick it up, get in it. What, do you want me to pick it up and come across your head with it? Mercy said.

You'll be alright Perry.

Yeah man. You'll be alright.

Then I heard knocks on the door.

"Hey man, come on, come on. Open up, open up."

What was that all about? I wondered. Unable to explain the moment I got up and walked to the door. Saxon said, "Sup, I want to go to Spelman's party and check out your cousin. Come on and ride with a brother."

"Dude are you kidding? I'm chilling. I am not going to no party."

He begged and pleaded and got on my nerves until the next thing I knew I was standing in a block party for Spelman and Morehouse. It was crowded and a beautiful shade of black folks everywhere. And just when I was about to turn around and tell Saxon that I wasn't feeling the environment I ran into Savoy.

"My brother told me he was coming to this thing with you. I couldn't believe it. You didn't want to hang out with me, but you wanted to party."

I should have asked him if he told his sister about the two of us going out, but I was still so baffled by my encounter with the angels that I wasn't thinking straight.

"Well, you go on and have some fun. Allen and I are sure gonna."

And then the basketball star from Tech that had violated her at the end of last year began putting his hands all over her.

"Wait, wait. What's this? You know what he's all about. Come on, Savoy. You don't want to be with me?"

"Well, at least he knows what he wants. And he has apologized ten times over for being too forward. He never stops calling me, so why shouldn't I give him a chance? I thought we had something before but I guess I was wrong. I guess we're both running from love."

~ 11 ~

Circling the Wagons

I *don't know Lord; I guess I am a little angry at you. Here I am trying to do it Your way and I still feel empty. One day I'm happy, the next day I'm pissed. I lose my girl; I don't hang out with my friends; I try not to be tempted. I mean, it's just one thing after another. It's a circle that I am sick of being a part of.*

I don't know why I was so angry. We were in the middle of Spring ball and on the field I was throwing down, but the reporters were all in my face, talking about how much of a screw-up I was. I wasn't even legally able to drink, how could the media think that college guys could handle all of their negative criticism? The fact that Coach Red wasn't taking up for me wasn't making me feel any better. Though he wasn't on the bandwagon with the press, he certainly didn't take a stand and have my back. All I knew was to show up on the field. But when Saxon showed up to make those same cuts, either he wasn't fully healed from his injury earlier in the year or the guy just didn't have it anymore. I couldn't believe it when he got up in my face and I was just doing my thing.

I didn't know what his problem was. Did he still have a beef with me or was he upset with his poor performance? Maybe it was both. I didn't want a confrontation, so I left. I got in my car and just wanted to drive. I had no particular destination, but I headed east on Interstate 20 out of downtown Atlanta. My cell phone rang and it was Payton. We hadn't talked in a while even though she'd been trying to reach me, and a big part of me didn't want to talk at that moment. Honestly I didn't have anything to say, but if she was calling then maybe she did.

"Hey sis, what's up?"

"Awh! I'm so glad I got in touch with you."

Sometimes when she had panic in her voice it just was annoying, I mean was it really all that or was she just exaggerating? And without just getting straight to the point, she talked round and a round about how many times it took her to get in touch with me.

"Look, I have football practice. I know Tad is up there working out too."

"I know, I know. I'm just saying it seems like if you saw that I called you that you would get right back to me," she said with an attitude. When I didn't respond she said, "Okay, okay. I'm just stressed because it's Dad."

I've always known my father to be a rock. So never had I known my sister to say that.

"What's going on with him?"

"He won't go get his colon checked."

"WHAT? Girl, you trippin'."

"No wait, Perry. This is serious. This is a big deal. He just turned fifty and he's supposed to go get it checked; actually he should have had it checked at forty. So he's already ten years behind and he won't go. Colon cancer is the fastest growing disease among African American males."

"Girl, you know how strong Daddy is. And isn't that thing hereditary?"

"That's my point. Granddaddy had colon issues."

"I didn't know that," I said.

"So anyway, will you just call him and talk to him?"

"I can't convince him to go see no doctor, you know how stubborn he is."

"This is our father and I know you're at Tech and life is great and all, but take your head out of your butt and care for someone else for a change. You need to be focused on Dad's behind, okay?"

"Wait, why it got to be all that? You trying to make it seem like I'm something special or whatever. You know me better than anybody. Why you gon' front on me like that?"

She was quiet, and the more I thought about it, the more pissed I got. "Well, shucks. If you going to accuse me of having a big head and all of that stuff then why don't you just handle all of that then? Keep me out of your scheme to get Dad to go to some doctor."

"Perry, wait, wait," she said, but I hung up.

For real, I had my own issues. My dad was a grown man. If he didn't want to go to the doctor then that was on him. I'm sure he was fine. He didn't have any signs of having an irritable bowel, and the way mom talked about him stinking up the bathroom didn't seem like he would have any problems with his colon. Though I didn't know what the symptoms would be like, being that I wasn't that educated on the disease. I just was feeling a little bit overwhelmed. I had never hung up on my sister before. But shoot, you grow up and you grow apart. I pressed harder on the accelerator and instead of driving at 70 mph like the sign had requested, I was going 90. My sports car could roll, and I started weaving in and out of Atlanta traffic. One guy put his middle finger up at me and that just made me press the accelerator even more. Was I losing my mind? Was I trying to crash? The clouds ahead were dark, and in two miles I was in rain. The traffic ahead of me was backed up. All I saw was red lights. I was going too fast to brake effectively and my car started skidding to the left. I grabbed the steering wheel tighter but lost control and went over to the right. To avoid hitting the eighteen-wheeler in front of me I skidded off the median and down an embankment. I opened my eyes, I took deep breaths. I couldn't believe I had come away unscathed. My car had stopped literally inches from an oak tree. I wasn't even stuck in the mud. I gained my composure and drove down to the left, which put me on some side street. I was in Covington.

I realized I was near the cemetery where my grandparents were buried.

In my mind the Goodness spirit said, *Alright, do you want to end up here now?*

Then Mercy came on the scene and said, *I thought you wasn't going to say anything to him. Obviously that is what he wants. Let him be stupid.*

I couldn't even remember where we put my grandparents. I hadn't been back out here since we put my grandmother in the ground, but as the raindrops hit my face I found their place and dropped to my knees, remembering when my father had his dark night and wanted to take his life. Maybe depression was hereditary.

Stick with God! Goodness said.

He don't think God cares, Mercy replied.

I looked up at the sky and pictured my grandparents way up over me holding hands and saying, *We know this ride of life is crazy boy, but just hold on.*

"I don't know if I can," I said honestly and then placed my head in the grass. I wept.

* * *

God's grace got me back to my apartment and even though I was emotionally drained, when I got in the door Lance and Deuce got all up in my face. It reminded me of when my dad got home and Payton and I would out-talk each other, both trying to get his attention. Whatever they were excited about destroyed my foul mood. I had no time to be bitter. I had to hear them out. So I said "Okay, okay. One at a time," almost laughing at their jovial expressions.

"Don't talk too loud," Deuce said.

"Yeah, yeah. He might hear us," Lance said.

Now both of them were acting real weird. Only the three of us lived here, and I did not feel like fooling with anybody. I had told them both to talk one at a time, but they kept talking to each other and talking to me at the same time. So I turned around and acted as if I was walking back out the door and Lance pulled me back into the room.

"Alright, alright. Deuce, you tell him. You left early from practice, man."

"I didn't leave early from practice. Coach dismissed us."

"He dismissed us from practice but we had meetings. You weren't the only dude who left so he wasn't tripping or nothing. You'll never guess who walked out on the field and showed everybody that he was back in full form."

"Back in full form," I said, completely confused. All of a sudden a dude that I hadn't noticed came forward from the back of the room.

"Collin!" I said, real excited.

"Perry, hey!"

I shared an embrace with Collin. The last time I had actually seen him in our place he was fighting for his life. He had left Tech after being released from the team. Lance, Deuce and I never thought we would see him again and here he was. I stood back to stare at him and then said, "So what, what you doing here?"

"I don't know, I just thought about a lot of the stuff we talked about. Never quitting, always finishing a job. I went to Alabama and thought about my life."

"So, what did you find?" I said, placing my hand on my hip and looking at him sternly. He choked last football season and then because of his poor performance he wanted to take his own life. Now he was back.

"I know I haven't come full circle and Coach Red hasn't given me my scholarship back, but I'm here as a walk-on. I went out there and he started me from the ten—and I went out there and kicked it through the upright. I moved back to the twenty—through the upright. Moved back ten yards until I got to the sixty—and again I kicked it through the upright."

"Yeah, Perry. He kicked it through every time." Lance came over as fired up as he could be to tell me the story.

Deuce came over and said, "Man you should have seen it. We all were tripping, none of us could believe it. The boy has been practicing down there in Alabama. He is bad!"

"Though the semester is almost over I'm going to be going to school this summer, but I can continue training, so since nobody lived in here . . ."

"We'd be glad to have you back; you don't even have to finish it. Dang man, it's good to see you."

"It's something, Perry, when you get a second chance," he said to me. "Trust me, I know what you're talking about. I just want to do it better this time." Collin looked at the three of us and confessed, "I don't want to let any of y'all down, but I don't want to let myself down either. I felt like the only way to go forward in life was to face my past."

The four of us decided to go down to the Varsity to stuff down some hamburgers and French fries to celebrate. When Lance and Collin got up to go, Deuce got up out of his chair and said to me, "What's up, man? I've been seeing Savoy out with the basketball dude. You put her down? You know Jailyn's been talking."

"Just cause everything is alright in your camp doesn't mean I can keep mine together. Be excited things are good for you, it is what it is for me and Savoy, you know?"

"Whatever, man, play that on somebody who don't know you. I know you like that girl, and her brother is so hot about her hanging out with the guy who sexually assaulted her."

"I don't have nothing to do with that. I tried to check her on that and she put me in my place. You only got to check me once, you know what I'm saying?"

"Come on, Perry, if you was doing your thing with her she wouldn't even be tripping like that. Why you be pulling away? You do the same thing with me. We supposed to be boys and yet you keep this thing sea level, we ain't going ocean deep no more, it's like that?"

I bit my lip. I was real uncomfortable Deuce had called me out. I didn't know why I was pulling away from everybody I cared about—my sister, my girl, my boys—but before I could get on the defensive Deuce lightly jabbed me in the shoulder and said, "But you know I've been praying for you, right dog?"

At that moment I was all choked up with emotion. He was praying for me. Maybe prayers are what allowed me to get back home. Maybe our prayers for Collin are what allowed him to get himself together and come back to Tech and show out. Maybe praying more was what would help to straighten out all of my insecurities. I just shook my head.

"It's cool man, why you think I was hitting the bottle? To be honest, man, I know where you are. You've got a lot going on, Perry. It's hard to walk in my shoes, but I couldn't imagine what it would be like trying to run around in yours. There's a God up there that loves the both of us and if He can help me keep it on the road don't stop giving Him a try.

Sometimes it's just like I'm going in circles and nothing gets better, but that's just it. You're going and you haven't stopped. He's the wind that is pushing you forward and when He gets ready, He'll straighten your course out. You've just got to trust Him."

I bit my lip again. I couldn't even look at my friend, but his words of wisdom ran deep, and silently I said, *Yeah, I've just got to trust Him.*

The week flew by. After all of the hard practice learning the new schemes the offensive coordinator had planned to incorporate next season, it was time for the Spring ball game. The only things that I had been focused on were my studies and the trio combination that proved to be a deadly one for the defense. Not only was I studying my playbook, I was acing my courses. But the biggest thing that proved to be powerful was getting into the Bible. My mind was starting to clear up. I really claimed the passage, *Greater is He that is in me than he who is in the world*. Every time I took my eyes off of God and started focusing on myself and my problems, my drama things spiraled out of control. I kept Him first and I was able to keep my eyes on the prize and be an overcomer. I was running circles around the defense. Coach Red had me running from the slot, running from the exposition and the Y. Wherever I was posted I was dominant. The throws from my roommate, quarterback Lance Shadrach, didn't hurt at all either. Deuce had even run an eighty-yard play. When the game was over I dropped to my knees. Too many cameras were on me but I prayed, not for show but because I was thankful.

You haven't given up on me. I know I take You through it giving You the praise and then doing stupid stuff, but Your Holy Spirit lives deep inside my soul. Some way, some how, I always find my way back to You. I appreciate this ability You have given me to dominate in athletics but show me what You want me to do with it. I'm tired of being blind doing it my way; Lead me, please?

As soon as I got up my teammates mauled me. The pile was so deep you would have thought it was the real game and we had just won the Super Bowl. Once we were all up Markus, the defensive lineman, a fifth-year senior, came up to me and said, "You are definitely the man, Perry Skky Jr. You are definitely the man. Let's do something tonight, man. What we gon' do?"

"Yeah, let's have a party," Saxon said as he came over to us. Both of them knew I wasn't feeling it. Saxon turned to Markus and said, "I'm throwing the bash."

Later on that night while I was relaxing in my room, Deuce came in and said, "You going over next door or what?"

"Man, there ain't nothing going on across the hall that either one of us needs to be a part of. There is going to be a bunch of alcohol, a bunch of females."

"Come on, man."

"There's nothing but trouble over there, right."

"Come on, we can pop our heads in for a second—dang, can Christians celebrate?"

I couldn't believe he was asking me that question. It wasn't a week ago that he was in my ear encouraging me to do the right thing and put God at the forefront of it all. Quicker than the blink of an eye he had switched. I had jeans on and a T-shirt. He threw my shoes at me and motioned for me to follow him. As soon as I walked into Saxon's, the smoke from something other than a cigarette consumed me.

"So this is what you wanted to be a part of?" I said sarcastically to Deuce.

"You ain't kidding, half these dudes in here look like they on something."

"Look like?" I said to him. "Let's be truthful now."

When we walked into the room a little bit more I was

somewhat relieved because most of the guys were not our teammates. It was a room full of brothers and a bunch of honeys but some of the guys looked unfamiliar. Then the more and more I stared at them I knew 'em. I wasn't trying to be overtly rude or nothing but this one guy I recognized. I had seen him before, and it was like my mind was playing tricks on me, seeing flashes of something horrific. I remembered seeing that dude that Mario shot down, and another car drive-by that scared the heck out of both of us. T-Money's crew was up in Saxon's place! They had admitted that they were excited that their leader was gone. The illegal drugs that Mario was a part of were now right across from where I lived and they brought that mess up here. I wished I had a siren and could scare them all into thinking that the cops were on their way, but I didn't have the balls to say that that stuff was messing their lives up. The guy with the dreads that I kept looking at walked over to me with an angry face like, *You got a problem with me?* My arms were folded and I didn't flinch.

"Mario told us to meet him here. He said the party was here and we got invited. It wasn't like we bust up in here or nothing. You looking at us like only the college dudes can be enjoying the honeys. We don't sell no more."

This was my chance to be used by God, to stand up for what was right, when the guy pushed me back a bit, wanting a response from me. He snapped his fingers in the air and his crew gathered round.

Deuce said, "Hold up now." As the football players gathered behind me, I wondered how I was going to play this out now that I had the attention of everyone in the room. Could I keep my promise to God now that He had put me on a stage to make a change? Could I reach down deep and give them all a dose of reality? Drugs, booze, promiscuity. They'd all be headed straight to Hell if they wouldn't stop circling the wagons.

~ 12 ~

Spreading God's Word

The dude took the joint out of his mouth and then shoved me again. I knew everyone was staring at us intensely. I knew my football teammates had my back. Quite honestly, looking at the crew's scrawny out-of-shape tails I knew we could beat them, but I didn't know if they were packing a piece, and for me the last thing I wanted was for violence to erupt. I put my hand firmly on his chest and said, "Man, get back."

"Straw, man, you gon' let him handle you like that?" someone said.

We knew his name on the crew finally.

Markus, my boy on the team, said, "Shoot man, he the straw, we the bricks. Y'all don't want no piece of us."

I turned to him and said, "Man, I got this for real."

Somebody yelled from the back, "Fight in the house!"

"No, no. It ain't gon' be no fighting."

Markus leaned into me and said, "Man, please don't preach. They need a beatdown."

"Like yo' fat short self is going to do something to somebody," Straw said to Markus.

"Oh, Perry, man, move out the way, I got this."

"Okay, hold up man! Hold up. I just want to say something and then y'all can do whatever y'all want to do." Looking around at all the angry faces I prayed, *Lord, I want to tell all these angry brothers about You. Give me the words to say. I need the words that won't back down, for all of those in front of me, help me be like Joshua and knock it down.*

"What's up? You wanted our attention," Straw said, stepping up in my face again. "What you got to say?"

"There's more to this life than living and dying. We care about our honor and no one wants to get punked, and you already saw one of your own die in front of your face. Being on this earth is not all that it's about and sooner or later we all are going to die. Yeah, it may seem like we're tough; smoking weed, drinking, getting high, banging girls, slinging cash. All that may give you a quick rush, even being a football player and being on that field might give you a rush," I said as I turned around and looked at my teammates. "Maybe a spot on the team is what you're seeking, but nothing can satisfy you like the love of God."

"Ha! Whatever, man, ain't nobody trying to hear that," Straw said as he turned around, but I dashed in front of him and made him look me in the eye.

"If you died tomorrow, Straw, can you honestly say you will be with God or do you think you will burn in Hell? You think having no money and no honeys is a horrible way to exist? Try darkness and damnation."

"Whatever man, God can't do nothing with me. So I ain't trying to hang out with Him."

"That's just the thing, God doesn't condemn. He doesn't even care about your past. Actually, if you read the Bible, the more screwed up your life is the happier He is to change it."

"Why you love Him so much?" Markus came over and asked. "You Perry Skky, for real you got it going on without Him."

"Naw, bro let's get it right. I am who I am because of Him. Any day He can take away my athletic ability. I could be in a car accident and my mind could get screwed." I hit my chest. "But, what's on the inside though? What's in my heart is what saves me and what gives me life. I knew He didn't just send me here to play ball. Yeah, it's a gift. I like it, it's cool, but I want to be able to talk to that dude to tell him about the Lord so he wouldn't be thinking that I was just—"

"Man, I ain't ready for a church service," some of Straw's boys said. They got their brown paper bag and headed to the door. "Straw, you coming?"

The door opened from the other side. It was Mario. He said, "Man, where y'all going?"

I quickly went over to Mario and said, "How you gon' invite them here bringing all of this crap?"

"Man, what are you talking about?" he said, clearly having no clue as to what I was talking about. I pointed to the joint on the floor.

"Wait, wait, wait! Who brought all of this in here? Aw, Straw, come on, man. I told you I wanted you to come and hang out with my boys at Tech, not bring stuff to get them in trouble. If you had to bring that then you shouldn't have came, man, dang. I know I'm late, but I'm holding down a little pizza job, but it's a good thing because I got food. Naw, man, I didn't want you to bring all of that around my boys. They could end up losing their scholarships."

"It's not your place though," Saxon said, entering into our conversation.

"Do you really want all of this in here?" I looked at him boldly and asked, "Did you hear anything that I have said, do you care about your life for real? I mean you were almost out of here lying in the hospital, technically dead. Now that you're back and with us you want to throw all of that away?"

Saxon just looked at me. We had never talked about his experience being in a coma; but obviously it was one that had shaken him up a bit. So, I wanted everybody in the room to grab each other's hands and say "I Love God," but I knew realistically that just wasn't going to happen.

Deuce then came up behind me and said, "I have never been the same since the Lord came into my soul. I ain't never had no daddy and since He and I have been tight I ain't wanted for nothing. All I have to do is get on my knees and pray and before I get up it's like He provides peace. Even when I didn't think I could quit hitting the bottle He gave me a way out. Listen to Perry y'all. What he's saying is real. You ain't tried God for yourself." He just shook his head and walked off.

So I jumped back in and said, "Y'all ain't trying to free yourselves? What you got to lose in trying?" I turned around and walked out after Deuce. I felt good that they had heard the Gospel. I had to let God do what He was going to do with them.

"You know my dad's an atheist?" Collin said to me as we worked out in the gym. The weights slid out from under my hands and the 400-pound bar hit my chest.

"Hey man, you alright?" Collin said as he pulled up the bar to help me from crushing my abs. I sat up and grabbed a drink of my water. "You heard what I said, right?"

"Yeah, I heard you. Man, I know that's got to be tough having a dad with that view. But what about you?" I asked, shooting straight to the point. "You think there is a God?"

I liked Mr. Cox a lot, and though we never talked about our faith, I didn't perceive him to be someone who didn't believe in God. He didn't look like, act like, talk like any of that.

"Lance and I have been talking about this a lot," Collin admitted as he sat on the other side of the bench press. "See, when you know a lot of men who go to church and they are sleeping around on their wives, not paying taxes, beating up their children, they seem so hypocritical. For the longest time I definitely didn't see a reason for me saying that I wanted to be like that. I thought they were all fake, and if they were representing a God that was good and allowed you to prosper and you still were doing cruel things, why would I think He was real?"

I sat back and listened to Collin make complete sense.

"Someone told me a long time ago that the only Jesus someone will see is the Jesus in you, and for most Christians, even me, it's hard to live the right way. Unfortunately when we sin we bring down His name. My mom, though, is a Catholic. How she got with my dad is probably the main reason I don't spend time with any of my grandparents. It divided our families."

"Yeah, I see how," I said.

"She and I have been talking more since I got home. It didn't matter how I was living my life before, I just wanted it to be all over. But when I survived, she opened up to me and told me that I had another chance. The Lord had spared me for some reason. My mom never talked to me about God at all; my dad wouldn't allow her to raise me that way. But when she thought she lost her son, she came to me so purely and she asked me to seek out my salvation for myself." He started looking heavenward. "God, if you're up there I don't want to be empty anymore. I don't want to be in a place where I am so desperate that I try to harm myself with pain. Aw, what am I doing, You're not real."

I quickly got up off the bench and went to him. "Oh yes, He is real and He hears you. In order to have a relationship with Him all you have to do is ask."

I felt the devil in the room playing tricks on us both, circling around us saying, *Nana nana. He's not going to become saved. Say what you want to Perry, it's not going to work. You might as well quit. He is mine.*

So I started saying more and more about why he needed

Christ. I was so fired up I was determined to win, and before our time was up Collin had dropped to his knees. We were two grown men with watery eyes praying for God's grace to save him.

Later that evening we made our way back to our apartment to find that Rev. Shadrach, Lance's dad, was visiting.

"Boys, it's good to see you both," the Reverend said.

I couldn't stop smiling because my friend had accepted Christ today. With all the sorrow I had felt when someone died in front of me who didn't know the Lord at all, I felt immense joy in a man reborn.

"I know you men have been through a lot. The pressures of college life, the demands of your athletics, I'm sure girls are thrown in there somewhere. I've been praying for you daily and I just felt like I needed to come up here and let you guys know that there is a God in Heaven that is about all four of you. Lance, He wanted me to tell you to give Him more." His son looked away; I could tell he was humbled in that he knew he needed to give God his best. "Deuce, I've been knowing you since high school. You made a bold proclamation with Him recently and He's proud." Deuce hit me on the shoulder, nodding his head. He did take a bold stance. "And Collin. He's glad to have you as one of His children."

I was never one that was big on prophecy but everything the Rev. Shadrach was saying was accurate. Then he turned around and looked at me.

"He told me to tell you, son, don't give up telling the lost about who He is. Some you immediately win for Christ, and some it may take a while. But what you're doing now, telling young men and women how much they need Him, He's called you too." He looked at all four of us and said, "God will never leave you or forsake you. You may not agree with

His methods but His love is higher and His ways are pure. Don't stop following Him and don't stop telling others, because whether you have been with Him for a day or all your life, He's enough." Rev. Shadrach got his keys, opened up the door and left.

Collin leaned back on the sofa and said out loud, "He's enough." The rest of us nodded but kept silent. I was truly thankful God sent us a word. That was enough.

It was Easter weekend and I was home. Damarius had asked Cole and myself over to his apartment. Honestly, I had no gut feeling about what could be going wrong, but I did know he sounded serious. Before I had dinner with my family I headed over to his place.

"Hey boy!" Cole said as soon as I got out of my car.

"What, you didn't go in?" I asked.

"Naw man, I was waiting on you. He sounded all scared and stuff, I don't know what he wants to tell us."

"How long you been waiting out here?"

"Not long, about forty minutes."

"Boy, I know you ain't been waiting this long."

"Seriously, I can't deal with this stuff. You always have the right things to say. He might need prayer or something—what am I going to say?"

"Cole, you know the Lord. You don't talk to Him now?"

"I say the Lord's prayer, you know, before football games and stuff. I don't even know none of those fancy words. He wouldn't even understand me."

"Cole, the Lord is not like that. Whatever you want to say to Him, He already knows what's in your heart. He just needs you to surrender yourself to Him so He can act."

He just looked at me and took it all in. God was a good God and He loved us. I don't know why everybody thought

He was so unapproachable. He was all knowing, all powerful and all superior and stuff, but He had His eye on the sparrow. He could read your heart even if no words were uttered.

"Bout time y'all got here!" Damarius said, opening the door before we even knocked. "A brother could be dying and his boys would take forever to come over and see about him."

"Aw man, but we're here," Cole said, walking in the door.

We went into the bedroom and I flashed back to my first drunk experience. It was our senior year and he punked me into drinking; it was one beer after another and the next thing I knew I was on his bed feeling like my heart was about to beat out of my chest. The place was eerie to me, but I tried to block that out and focus on him. Damarius was twiddling his thumbs and Cole was looking at the ceiling. What was all of that about? Damarius called us over here; he needed to get right to the point so I said, "Alright, we're here now. What's up?"

"I'm going to war. I enrolled into the army."

I was speechless. I couldn't believe what I had just heard him say.

Cole sat up and said, "Naw man, you ain't doing that, it's not our war to fight."

"I already enrolled, Cole, so chill, man. My cousin up north—you know my family that I went to see when Ciara died?"

"Yeah," I said finally speaking, "what about them?"

"Well, he just died over there I want to go get payback."

"Are you feeling okay?" Cole said as he went over to try and lay his hand on Damarius' forehead. Of course Damarius slapped it off.

"I'm fine, I'm fine. I know what I have to do. It's a family thing, plus I want to protect our homeland."

"Damarius, people are really killing people over there,

man. You just talked about your cousin. You're in school—why would you let that all go to go join the army?"

"I told my cousin that if anything ever happen to him while he was in the army that I would go and defend his honor. But I'm going to be honest with y'all, y'all my boys and have been since grade school. I'm a little nervous."

"When do you head out?" I asked.

"I leave tomorrow and only for a month, but I just wanted to wait until you guys came home for the holidays. Really, I don't want anyone to talk me out of it. I know once I get there I'll do my thing. School wasn't for me, I do want a purpose to my life. I just wanted to ask you Perry, what if I don't make it over there? What's going to happen to me?"

I had talked about God for the last couple of years. We had got into it so badly that I had vowed never to bring it up again and now he was asking me what I thought would happen to him if he went to fight on foreign soil and didn't return.

"I don't know what you did when it came to your salvation Damarius, but I know you have to make sure that it is secure. We never know when our last day is. Cole and I could leave and get into a car accident, though it is unlikely. But when you go off to war the risk of death becomes heightened. So you just need to make sure your house is in order, and I don't mean financially and all of those things. I know the government has stuff in place for all of the soldiers, but I'm talking about your heart," I said as I looked my friend in the face. I put my index finger straight into his chest. "Does God know you? Is your name written in the Lamb's book of Life? If a bullet went through you and caused you to never breathe on this side of Heaven again, would your soul move on?"

The three of us were becoming emotional, but we held back the tears. The reality was that what Damarius was about to do was dangerous. But as we held hands and got on our knees and prayed Damarius said, "God, I don't know if I know who You are or not. I know I pray to You sometimes and I know there are times when I am so angry with You, please just forgive me. Know that I need You in my life and I want to be with You in Heaven."

I didn't like the fact that I basically had to come over to my friend's house to say goodbye, but if this is what it took to make sure he knew God, it was well worth it, spreading God's word.

~ 13 ~

Pouting for Sure

"Where in the world have you been?" my sister screamed at me as soon as I got out of my car at my folks' house on Easter Sunday.

"I told y'all I would be right back, dang," I said, not wanting to give her the same attitude she was obviously giving me. But a brother was saddened about the news of his friend departing for overseas. She didn't want to mess with me at that point, but when I tried to get around her she stood in front of me. "Payton, come on now. I'm trying to change out of this suit."

"We've been waiting here for you for two hours; you said you would be right back, Perry. Does everything have to be around you all of the time?"

"Y'all could have ate if that is what this is all about. Obviously something came up and I was there for someone else. It's not about me, I'm tired of you always alluding to that, girl, dang. I remember you bossing me around when we were little but if you haven't noticed, I tower over you now."

I glared at her, and when she wouldn't move I shoved her slightly out of my way, letting her know that I did have power. I wasn't playing with her. She was away at college just like me, and when she was at home she was spending time with Tad, so she really wasn't home that much, either. So now, just because I was away for a little longer than she thought was okay, I had to get the third degree.

But before I could step in the house she said to me, "Dad has cancer, okay."

I put my hand on my head and rubbed it a bit. I couldn't move. Surely she didn't say what I thought she said. I know it had been a while since I had talked to my parents and I had just come up this morning for church, and my dad had asked me via voicemail to come as soon as I could. Was this what he had wanted to talk about? Was what Payton telling me for real? Did my dad have cancer?

"Hmm hmm. See, now you want to listen. I hate you Perry, I hate you. It's all your fault." She came over to me and pounded her fists on my chest. "I told you a month ago that we needed him to get tested and you wouldn't help me. He waited, and maybe he waited too late, and now he has cancer."

I didn't budge. She was right. I had dismissed what she was saying then, and now I wished I would have believed her, I wished I would have helped, I wished I would have done more. Oh my Gosh, THIS WAS MY FAULT! I couldn't even hold my sister but I let her cry next to my heart.

My mom came outside and said, "Payton, you cannot stand here and say this is anyone's fault. Yes, early testing helps, but a few weeks ago? Come on sweetie, he should have gone in two years ago, five years ago at age forty-five. He's been stubborn for the longest time. Your father doesn't blame either one of you for this."

"Aw, Mom," Payton said, leaving my arms for my mother's. For some reason my mother was saying that it wasn't my fault, but whatever. I didn't even agree with her logic, how could I not blame myself? I hadn't been the best son; I had been consumed with my life, my friends' problems, my world, my drama. I could have made my parents a part of my world, but I had stepped away, I had pulled away. I had been every place but connected to them, and finally I showed up late and got the news that my father had cancer. If I was a super hero I would have torn the house down—that's just how bad I felt, that's just how angry I was. My mother and sister went inside and I just leaned my head up against the bricks. I looked up at the sky and I couldn't even manage to argue with the Lord. God was all powerful, all knowing. Here I was telling people how He would make things right, so why didn't He take care of my dad? I could see if I wasn't doing things His way, but I had been good, I had been strong—and then I felt someone touch my shoulder.

"Dad," I said, tearing up.

"So, you heard the news huh? Your old man has colon cancer. Your mother has been on me for years to go get checked, your sister started doing it too, and so I finally went, but sometimes you know that you know, but you don't want to hear the diagnosis. But you're looking like this is the end, son."

"You've got cancer Dad. I mean, that is what a lot of black men are dying from now. I just never thought that you . . . I mean . . ." I just reached over and hugged him. "How could God allow this to happen?"

"God has a reason and purpose for everything and I've got treatment options."

Treatment options. I walked over to the other side of my car and said, "Come on, Dad. I'm a big boy."

"No son, it's not a grim prognosis. I've got to have some chemotherapy and some radiation and some other stuff done, it's a fifty-fifty chance I'm going to be alright. Just because God doesn't give it to us how we want doesn't mean we give up on Him. At the end of the day we don't want to stay here forever."

"But Dad, didn't you just lose a high school friend last year?"

"It's not on our time, we have to trust and obey that God can work it out, not get mad and get angry and give up on Him when we disagree with His methods. And with this deep conversation that I am having with you now, maybe it is worth it. I missed you, son."

He walked straight to me.

"I missed you too."

"What's wrong with y'all? Y'all look like somebody just died," I said when I got back to my place and saw the defeated look on Deuce and Collin's faces as they sat somberly in the living room.

Deuce quickly came over to me. "It's Lance, man."

"What's wrong with Lance?"

"His family wanted him to go home for Easter and he didn't go, and he just got a call last night that his grandma died."

"Aw man, are you serious?"

"Yeah man, and he ain't taking it too well. We thought since you lost your grandma earlier that you would be able to say something to him."

"What happened to her?"

"She had a heart attack and didn't overcome it."

Collin came over and said, "We've been praying for him, but Deuce is right. He's been hysterical and won't talk to anybody. Clearly he's angry. You've got to be able to get through to him."

This day was just getting worse and worse. My drive back was full of thoughts that my dad might not make it, and even though God has to take us all, I'm not cool with that. So what could I say to Lance not being okay with the fact that his grandma is gone.

Dang it, Lord, I thought.

As I walked into my bedroom on the other side of our place, Deuce came in and said, "Unh-uhh, man, you need to go try and talk to him."

"I'm just not up to it right now, alright. If you want to talk to him then go talk to him. Sometimes a man just needs space. How can you expect me to do what you couldn't do?" I sat down quickly. "Quit being a punk and stop putting stuff off on other folks, dang. Leave me alone."

"Oh, well if it's like that then fine," Deuce said.

"Wait, wait, wait," I said quickly, coming to my senses. "I'm sorry man, I'm sorry."

"Whatever man, if you feel that way, cool. You talk about brotherhood and unity and all that stuff, but obviously that's not how you felt. Those were the words you spouted, not the ones you intended to live by. I'm glad I know now though."

"Naw, naw. Deuce, seriously. I'm sorry, man."

"How come you two are fussing now?" Collin said, entering the room.

"I just found out that my father has colon cancer, alright. I don't think I'm the best candidate to talk to him right now, alright. Lance ain't the only one that's going through stuff, that's all I'm trying to say. Maybe I was a little harsh with my words and I am sorry about that, Deuce, but I've got my own issues you know."

"Aw man, I didn't know, man. I'm sorry."

"Well, don't stay in your room and wallow and be alone and stuff," Collin said to me. "Deuce is right, we have to be here for each other. Y'all were here for me. When I wanted to give up on myself y'all were there for me. Come on man, let's go sit in the living room."

We all sat down on different sides of the living room. What was happening to me? My dad was right—when things didn't go my way I started to doubt my faith, when it should be tested to make me stronger. I was rebelling, going off on

Deuce like that. Although I had a reason, it was inexcusable. I didn't know what to say to Lance, but I knew that I did need to try and say something.

Without either Deuce or Collin saying anything to me, I got up off my tail and went to his room and banged on the door. When I didn't get a response I just talked, like when I had to talk to Lenard after he had found out that his aunt and uncle got killed in a car crash on their way to our game. Even then I didn't know what I was going to say, but God had given me everything I needed to help him out. Lance and I had a connection; just him knowing I cared was all I needed to share. So I said, "Listen guy, you probably want to be alone. I lost both of my grandparents and both times it affected me, it hurt me really badly. I still miss not being able to eat my grandma's chitlings and collard greens. But I still remember her loving the Lord and seeing her in Heaven is what sustains me, and God is sending others into my life—new family, so to speak. You and Deuce and Collin and I have a brotherhood. I don't know, it's real and it's strong enough to get us through the pain, and all we want to do is be there for you, guy. You can hit us, hug us, whatever—but you don't have to go through this by yourself. Let's pout together. Your world will be changed forever without your grandma and that ain't cool, but all that she made you to be, and the three friends you've got in this apartment, is something to hold onto. Come on man, let us in?"

It took a few minutes, but I finally heard footsteps walking to the door. Lance opened it, and Deuce and Collin were right behind me. We just smiled at him—after the pain was goodness.

A week later the Deltas were having a party on campus. Another reason why my sister and I weren't close was that my sister was on line. I wasn't going to go to the jam, but when she came down I went out to support her and see her step. Knowing how stubborn Payton Skky was, imagining her as a Greek was something I couldn't imagine. But seeing it for myself I was impressed that my sister had the fly moves.

"She's cute, ain't she?" Tad said, all proud and everything.

"She's your girlfriend, not mine," I told him. "You've got your hands full."

"I know she told me you two got into it when you were at home last weekend. Your dad's going to be alright, man."

"Thanks, Tad."

I just happened to look over to the left of the dance floor and I saw Jordan the basketball dude, who was supposed to be going out with Savoy, with his lips all over some other chick. Now I have to admit that the AKA was fly, but how he gon' disrespect Savoy like that and be with somebody else? No sooner had that dance ended than another girl grabbed his hand and he started feeling her up and down on the dance floor. Savoy didn't deserve that treatment at all.

"What's wrong with you?" Tad said, noticing that I looked ticked. I had forgotten Savoy was his cousin. Did I even want to get him involved in all that when part of me was mad at myself? Knowing that if I had done my job as her boyfriend she wouldn't have to be treated any kind of way by jokers who didn't respect her. But I couldn't cry over spilt milk. I still cared for her deeply and I was a man of action, but I didn't know what I was going to do until I saw him with yet another girl, kissing her in front of everybody. Yeah, he probably wasn't going to stay at Tech after his freshman year. Unlike football players, basketball players only had to come to school for one year, but for football they had to play at least three. So even though the both of us were supposed to do real well in the pros, he'd be seeing his green sooner than me, and the honeys were buying into the hype.

"I'll be back," I said to Tad.

"Man, I ain't going to be here. I've got to find your sister, you know how that goes. Parties aren't my scene at all, but we'll dance a minute and then we're headed out, so if we don't see you."

"Alright dude," we said as we slapped hands.

Then I lost Jordan. I looked to the left, he wasn't there. I looked to the right, he wasn't there. And then I saw Savoy. She was sitting in a corner by herself and she looked so sad, like she lost her best friend or something and desperately needed someone to rescue her from her gloom. I couldn't believe she was waiting on him to return. Had that ever been her nature? She never waited on me like that. Why would she reduce herself to that? And then I saw him go over to her and talk to her, and she started smiling. What in the world—she had to know that he was a jerk! This wasn't cool.

I went over to the two of them and said, "Unh uhh, wait Jordan. You ain't gon' front on my friend like that. You've been with three different honeys, I've seen you myself. Kissing on them, feeling on them, all of that stuff. And then you gon' try to come over to your girl and act like you've been an outstanding model guy. Naw, it ain't gon' go down like that. Savoy deserved way more than you."

Savoy's mouth was wide open and Jordan just started laughing. I thought he was going to be mad and say something to me, go off or whatever, but he was just laughing. Why didn't I get the joke? I knew what I saw, I wasn't making it up. She didn't even seem to be appalled by it, she was just sort of blushing. What was going on?

"Man, me and her ain't been together for a month—Savoy?" She nodded. "This girl is still into you and it's apparent that you're still into her. We friends though, she keeps it real and gets on me. She was just chastising me about the exact same thing, saying I'm too out there, so I have to come to her every now and then. It's just like you thought we were still together—it works with the girls too. Y'all need to work that thing out. It'll mess up my groove, but hey, y'all two good people. I couldn't get nowhere with your partner, she was still hooked on you. But you ain't gon' mess up my game with these other ladies, believe that. I'm out of here. Bye Savoy," he said, kissing her on the cheek. "You think people were looking?"

"Boy, get out of here."

"Is what he said really true?" I asked, sitting beside her. "I saw you looking sad, like you couldn't believe that he was doing you like he was."

"I wasn't thinking about Jordan at all but I was sad. I have been pouting lately because I miss you. So what can I do about that?"

"Tell a brother how you feel," I said as I held her hand.

"Would that do any good, Perry?"

"You know it would. I came all the way across a dance floor to go off on a guy that I thought was supposed to be true to you, all because I cared in the worst way. If you thought it looked cute, if it made you blush, if it makes you want to get back with me, it was worth the pouting for sure."

~ 14 ~

Feeling Real Joy

When her lips touched mine it was perfect; I felt so relaxed, so good, so on top of the world. I didn't want to pull away from her. And don't get me wrong, it wasn't about sex and satisfying an urge. No, it was more about the pigheadedness being gone. I stayed away from Savoy because I didn't want to admit that I could care so much for a girl, have her presence control my happiness like that. And truthfully, sometimes I didn't want to have to fool with her, but deep down, damn, all of that was worth it. Some way, somehow, that kiss taught me that we would find a way to coexist. There was no way we could be apart; and that every brother deserves someone who cares about him so much that no other guy even has a chance.

"I missed you," she said with watery eyes. "I never thought we could be together again. I mean we were together, not together, then apart."

"And now we are together," I said to her as I held her hand and brought her head toward mine. I mean, what was there to say—her lips could speak volumes.

I was so focused on the emotions I felt, kissing Savoy, that I was startled when my sister called out, "Perry!"

"Oh my gosh!" Savoy said when she opened her eyes and

saw her brother and cousin Tad looking at her with displeasure.

"I'm sorry. This is probably embarrassing, huh? Corner of a party making out . . . nah, we just came over to say it's about time you get out," her brother Saxon said, before he turned left.

Payton said, "You two got something special. Remember, Tad and I found a way to work it out as freshmen. Everybody in the world said there is no way that our relationship could work out, and we have had more than our share of almost-never-ever-gonna-stay-together moments. But Savoy, I know you care about my brother. Your cousin tells me you talk."

"Tad!" she said.

"Payton!" he said to her. "Well, I mean I'm saying."

My sister looked at me so I stepped in and said, "You talk to your cousin about you missing me and stuff?"

"Well, its not like I can talk to Saxon."

"Dude, you never told me," I said to my sister's boyfriend.

"Wasn't my place. Prayed for y'all though. Figured if it was supposed to work out it would. Like Payton said, y'all are young and not everybody can try to do what we doing. It ain't easy for us. But I know what is in Savoy's heart is real. And from what Payton tells me—let's just keep it real here—you moping around and all that other kind of stuff, and shucks—I can see for myself this whole night you was staring at my cousin."

"I was," I said, looking dead at her.

"So now that y'all got another chance, don't mess it up," Tad added.

Payton said, "People will try to break you up, and the feelings you'll have for each other will sort of mess up your commitment to God. You're going to be tested on so many fronts it's not even gonna be funny."

"Yeah I know, we've already been tested like that," Savoy said. "I just don't know if we can make it."

Well thanks y'all for the talk," I said, hearing enough. I grabbed Savoy's hand and we headed to the door.

"It's not too cold out, I wanna talk to you."

When we got outside I said, "I know we've been through a lot and I know I've been a jerk through a lot of it, but if you care about me the way I care about you we can make it."

I took my hand and stroked her beautiful hair, then she rested her head in the palm of my hand and I felt so in control, like she wanted me to take care of her. I didn't have it all together, I knew that I would mess up even more along the way, I couldn't say she would be my wife one day. But for right now I was willing to make her a promise that I would give her all I had. I didn't use the words *I love you* much. But I leaned in and gave her a kiss on the cheek and said, "Rest assured I'm in this. You won't leave my soul, Savoy Lee. I love you."

She hugged me tight and prayed, "Lord, so many nights I cried, missing Perry, hating myself that I had driven him away. But now You have given us new life on this dating journey and he says he loves me, and I love him too. Thank you God. This is what we are feeling; this passion; this excitement; this joy is a gift from You. Help us treasure it."

I said "Amen" in complete agreement.

Hadn't been the same around the apartment with Lance out of town in Arkansas for his grandmother's funeral, no TV blaring loud in the middle of the night, no refrigerator door wide open because he forgot to shut it. Nobody playing practical jokes on folks in the house but Collin, Deuce, and I did miss him.

"Maybe we should've gone to the funeral," Collin said as

we sat around our small dinette table eating our ramen noodles.

"Man, I couldn't go to no funeral in Arkansas. I got classes. You know I couldn't afford to miss nada one," Deuce said.

Collin said, "I mean, we should've been able to do something, has anybody even called him?"

Deuce said, "I thought one of y'all called him."

Collin replied, "Nah, I thought y'all called him."

I said, "Well, I didn't bug him because I thought you guys did."

"So nobody has even checked on him?"

"I mean, I prayed for him," I said.

"If somebody in my family died y'all better show up," Deuce said.

"Well," I got up and said, "where's the phone, let's call him now."

Then we heard the rattling of the doorknob.

"What y'all sitting here looking all sad for, y'all should've had more food for me to eat—what's the problem?" said Lance.

We got up to slap his hand and gave him small hugs.

"You appear to be okay," I said to him as I checked him out.

And Deuce gave him a wedgie, "Yeah he's alright."

"See, y'all got jokes," Lance said.

"For real, guy, we were thinking about you; sorry we didn't give you a call. It's not like we wasn't thinking about you and stuff," I said to him.

"You guys, I know I was a little weirded out before I left but it was actually a peaceful experience, and I was so busy with all my relatives that I wouldn't even have heard the phone ring if you called. I don't think I even checked the messages. My girl is even mad at me."

"Your girl? What's up with that?" Collin said, messing with him.

"Yeah, Perry here hooked me up with a chick. She got a few issues but I like her."

"You've gotta girlfriend now?" Collin asked in a way that told us he was a little jealous.

"I guess you can call her that," Lance said to him.

"Now I'm the only one without somebody, dang."

"Well if Perry could find somebody for that nut, certainly we can get you hooked up. The honeys are going to be lined up at the door," Deuce told him. "I'm sure he's got some sorority girlfriends, all of them are always looking for somebody."

Collin said in a depressed tone, "Yeah, but as messed up as it was for me, I was the talk of campus last semester with everything that happened with the ambulance and the hospital and me wanting to not . . . you know all that."

"Whatever, man, them girls got more drama, bulimia, more operations to add to this and that to take away from that and this."

"And then it's rape I threw in there," I said. Suddenly it got quiet and Lance looked at me.

"I need to see you now, NOW!!" he sort of yelled. He went to his bedroom.

Collin and Deuce looked at me like, "Man, what's up?"

I threw up my hands like I didn't know, and went into his room and shut the door.

"What's up man, you want to talk to me?"

"Why you said rape? Something been going on with Anna. Every time I touch her and stuff . . ." He turned crazy, grabbed me by my collar and threw me at the door.

"What you do to her, man?"

"Wait, wait hold up, hold up dude, hold up!" I said, pushing him off of me.

"What's going on in there?" Deuce asked.

"I got it y'all, I got it. Nah, I don't know if I do have it. Why would you say rape like that Perry? You know something . . ."

"Yeah, I know something, but it's not my business to tell you, alright, and no I didn't rape the girl, but some stuff happened to me before I came here and she's a part of it."

"I'm confused . . ."

"Lance, partner, I'm not going to go into it. You need to talk to her about all that. You need to let her know you really care. I don't know why she hasn't shared all that stuff. It's not my place to say, I was just bringing that up after you mentioned some other things that girls have to stress about . . . That's it. For you to think I did something to her, that really offends me."

"Alright alright, I'm sorry, it's just I really like her and I'm trying to break through all that, and I thought about it a lot and I thought about that at the funeral, you know? I want my life to count for something, I want my life to stand for something. So many folks said so many great things about my grandmother. And it's like her presence is with me and I want to make her proud, and part of that is settling down and caring for somebody the way she did for my grandfather. But I can't do that if Anna won't let me close. I don't know . . . I was wrong for thinking that . . . I'm sorry, I'm sorry," said Lance.

"We straight, it's definitely evident that you care for her, to try and jump me, what . . . My little roommate growing up," I said.

"Whatever," Lance said. "I care about her and I know it. She does make me happy."

"Then go for it, man," I replied. "We gotta find Collin somebody."

"You think we can?" Lance asked.

We both laughed.

* * *

It was dead week for students at Georgia and Georgia Tech, which meant there were no classes because it was time to study for exams. I couldn't believe my first year of college was almost over. I learned so much. I was challenged so much that I had became a tougher man. I learned to care about my brothers as myself. I learned I had to stand up for what was right. And I learned it was okay to give my heart to Savoy. Things might not always go my way, but I could survive it because God is on my side and though I didn't understand most of what He was up there doing, I certainly knew He had my back, front, sides and all. My angels, Goodness and Mercy, came to visit and the two of them didn't say anything, but I felt them encouraging me to call my sister and do something with my dad. He was being real tough going through the whole colon cancer thing. I didn't know a lot, and honestly didn't really have a desire to get into the ins and outs of the treatment. But one thing I knew was that I wanted my dad to be okay. And I knew he needed to know that I cared more than I could say.

So I dialed her up. "Perry what's going on? I was just heading to the library."

"I don't know sis . . . This is crazy, but maybe we should go home. I could be there in a couple hours."

"Yeah I could too . . . You know, after I pack up some things."

"You talk to Dad . . . Is there something I need to know?"

"No, no. Nothing like that. I just thought maybe we can go home, surprise him and mom and maybe make a weekend of it."

"How much room you got left on the credit card?"

"My Visa still has $2500. You?"

"The same."

"And they thought we would run their credit up," Payton joked. "What you thinking?"

"I don't know, maybe we swoop them up and go to Charleston or something for the weekend. All get massages, just be there for him. I don't know, what you think?"

"I think he'd like that . . . But will he take time away from the dealership?"

"With as many people over there and with all he's going through, we'll make it so he won't have a choice."

"Alright, I'll call Mom on the way," she said. "You . . . can work it out with Dad. What are you thinking, chartering the plane?"

"You got me."

"Sweet."

When I got home and went by the dealership, I noticed my dad had a new secretary. She looked more homely and older than my mom. I was so glad that the young chick that he had the little thing with was gone. Just for that alone I wanted to take him out and hug him.

But as he was fussing at some salesman for not meeting their quota, I knew it wasn't going to be easy to just pull him away. It was the end of the month, a Saturday was coming, he was going to make his hustle and I'm sure the business had been keeping his mind off the physical pain.

I was going to have to pull a fast one to get him to cooperate.

"Son, what are you doing here?"

I bit my tongue, knowing that I didn't want to freak him out but hoping the stress would be worth it in the end.

"Dad, we gotta fly up to Athens."

"Son, what's going on with Payton, where is my phone? WHERE IS MY PHONE?" he yelled out.

"Dad, Dad, it's all taken care of."

"What do you mean it's all taken care of? We gotta fly up to Athens and you're not making any sense, boy."

What could I say right then and there, something he could forgive me for? Something that would give him the urgency to move quickly forward.

"Payton is getting some sort of award from the school and their president has chartered something. I don't know, Dad. All I know is I'm suppose to escort you up there."

"For real? We have been invited by the president of the school? Your sister always had it going on, I tell you what . . . Where is your mom?"

"She is going to meet us at the airport."

About an hour later, Payton and my mom came to the airport too.

"Well, if Payton is here then how are we supposed to be going to . . . Perry!?"

My dad couldn't even finish his statement. He knew I was up to something.

"Where are we going?"

"Honey, the kids want to take you to relax for the evening. We're going to Charleston."

"And who's paying for it?"

"Dad, we got a deal," Payton said.

"Dad, we wanted you to get away from the hustle and bustle of everything and be with your family. You are going through a lot right now," I told him as we strapped in on the plane, preparing to take off.

"Son, I appreciate this, but I got a business to get back to. I'm okay." He starting unstrapping his seatbelt.

"No Perry Sr., you sit right there," my mom said. "You do deserve this break. I've been thinking about it for a while and I'm glad the children took the initiative. The kids love you, sweetie. Although they are off in their own worlds, they love their dad. And I love him too, and we need you to rest and enjoy your family so that you can heal."

My dad leaned back in his seat as the plane lifted up toward heaven and he said, "This has been a lot. You all just don't know. God's given me the strength to get through it and I'm supposed to get word soon on the results from the surgery. One good thing is the doctors think they got it all. But as I think on my lesson out of all of this, I realize that my life is not about selling cars. It's not even about my health. My true joy comes from being with you three. I'm a rich man. I've got a family that loves me, and it means a lot to me that you all are doing this. It's taken me a long time, but no matter what the results say, I am going to be okay. I finally understand what it is truly like feeling real joy."

~ 15 ~

Finding Our Way

I rushed in to the living room when I heard an irate man banging on our door, yelling, "Where is he? I need to see him right now! I'm looking for Collin! Open up now before I kick this door in. This is his dad and I said open up NOW!"

"Is that really his dad?" Deuce said to me. Both of us were a little confused as to why Collin's dad was outside showing his butt at 11:30 at night! Collin was dead to the world so he certainly couldn't tell us that his dad was coming. And even when he was in the hospital fighting for his life I don't recall meeting his dad, so I wasn't sure if the man outside was really related to him. In other words, I was hesitant to answer the door.

"Dang! Does somebody hear me?" The man continued to bang.

"I ain't letting him in," Deuce said, thinking the same thing I was. "Man, go get Collin."

"I know you're in there. I hear you on the other side of the door. Open up!"

"He's gon' break it down!" Deuce said.

"Collin! Collin, man. Get up. I think your dad's here," I said after I woke up our roommate.

"My dad? He's in Alabama," Collin said.

"Well, some man outside beating on the door is claiming he's your father. Whoever this man is we need to find out."

"He's beating on the door? It probably is my dad." Collin grabbed his jeans, threw them on, and sprang to the front door and opened it.

"Get your stuff and let's go now," his dad said without a word of hello. He ran into my room. "Get your stuff so we can go."

"Sir, that's my room," I said as Collin collapsed on the couch with his head between his knees.

"Son, where is your room so we can get your stuff and go?"

Deuce went over to him. "Man, what's going on? Why is he saying you have to leave?"

"Boy, you need to stay out of this!" Collin's dad said boldly. "Show me where your room is now!" Collin still didn't move. His dad stepped up to him, yanked him off the couch, and shoved him against the wall.

Lance was always a heavy sleeper but all this commotion woke him up. "Man, who's fighting?" Lance joked. Deuce and I gave him a look to let him know it wasn't funny. "Sir, you gotta let go of him." Lance stepped between Collin and his dad.

"Get back, Lance. I got this," Collin said as his dad grabbed Collin's neck.

I couldn't stand back anymore. I mean, that was his father and it seemed to be none of my business, but now it was. Why was he choking his son like this? "Sir, so I need to call the police?" I yelled out.

He let go of Collin and Collin grabbed his throat and started choking. Lance went to get Collin some water but he wouldn't take it.

"You gotta let me live my own life. I'm not going anywhere okay," Collin said to his dad, who had found Collin's room and was emptying the contents of his dresser drawers.

I was so confused. "What is going on? Why is he so pissed?" I said to Collin. "Explain this to me. You tell your father you're not leaving but yet in the middle of the night he said you have to. He said some comment about God."

"There it is. You hit it right on the head. I told you my dad is an atheist. My mom probably told him that I'm a Christian. I knew when he found out it wasn't going to be pretty."

"Alright, son, let's go. Let's go," he said carrying a ton of clothes wrapped in Collin's sheets. "You're all done here. We can get the rest of your stuff later."

"Dad, I'm not going anywhere. You can beat me, push me, choke me, hit me, do whatever. You can try to get me to say I don't love God but I do, Dad. I've looked at it your way all my life, as if the Lord doesn't exist. I've seen Him work miracles. I've seen Him change my heart."

"It's these guys, Collin. If I can get you away from these guys you'll be fine."

"It's not the guys that I'm serving, Dad. If I'm not around them, I'm still going to love God and know that there is a Jesus that died on the cross for our sins. I'm still going to know that the Holy Spirit is going to give me the power to stand up to a dad that bullied and beat me all my life. I can't even say I love you for the way you treated me for most of my upbringing. But I can say I forgive you for the way you treated me and Mom."

"Collin, if you don't come with me now, don't you ever come back to Alabama. Unless you get this foolishness out of your system I won't claim you as my son."

Collin walked over to the front door and held it open. His father walked through it, dropping the bundle of Collin's clothing. The four of us just stood there, shaken by the whole scene. We knew sometimes following Christ could cost us everything. I was glad I didn't have to make a choice to forget my family because of it, but Collin did and I admired him wholeheartedly. There was a God in Heaven and as I knew now, I was going to have to be Collin's family. I could only pray that his dad would come around, and even if he didn't Collin had found his way. Heaven was pleased. Heaven was pleased.

The next day I woke up at five in the morning. I heard someone scrambling around in the kitchen. After the night we'd just had I couldn't ignore it. Maybe Collin's dad had come back. Maybe someone couldn't sleep. I just didn't know. I got up and found Collin fixing coffee.

"Hey, man. Are you okay? I know you're not as hard a sleeper as Lance but five in the morning? Talk to me. I know what happened. The confrontation with your dad threw you off, I know. We can talk about anything."

"No, Perry. I'm really okay. I'm just trying to have some quiet time with the Lord. I'm not stressed. I'm not falling apart. I'm not upset. I'm following Him now. He's making it okay now."

"The thing with your dad is over. We're boys; we can talk."

"Yeah, I know we are. I'm not trying to act tough. I just turn that over to God so it can work out. I can't fix everybody in the world. I can't even fix my pops. He hurt me so much in growing up, and he can't hurt me anymore so I'm rejoicing now, so I can get even stronger, you know. Don't think I'm cruel or that I've written my dad off like he said he wrote me off, but God wants us to be equally yoked. How can I stay on the straight and narrow if I allow my dad's negativity toward Him to be in my way? You know what I'm saying? I'm falling in love with Jesus."

I sat there and listened to him. And I went over to the cupboard to get myself a mug. I needed to have myself some quiet time too. I needed to know more about Collin's faith so I could fall more in love with Him myself. Collin had just accepted the Lord weeks before this, but yet he was excited and had a passion that was contagious. Not even his dad wrapping his bare hands around his neck, choking him, could set him back. I needed to be set on fire like that! So we sat down, opened up God's word together, prayed, drank our coffee, and felt renewed. I was determined to have more days start like that. God had given me so much. I wasn't going to be able to save the world. I wasn't going to be able to fix everybody. I was certainly excited that He could fix me. How good it felt to rejoice.

I had to head down to Augusta to sit with my folks as we awaited the results of my dad's cancer treatment. And as I drove up there I had more time to think about my relationship with God. I prayed, *Lord, I know I let You down so many times before and I ask for so much. Sometimes You say no and sometimes You say yes. Help me to be excited about Your plan for my life. Help me to see that path You have set for me. I'm not naïve, Lord. As a young black man I now see it's hard as a college athlete, trying to live up to expectations. As a guy in love it's not going to be easy doing the right things, so I just need You in my life to help me stay strong.*

I listened to a CD and it helped me to praise God. It wasn't about me wanting something from Him. It wasn't even about thanking Him. It was simply about praising Him. God was bigger than all my problems. He even knew how many hairs were on my head. I wanted to eventually dwell with Him and in order for that to happen I had to live right here. It wasn't a question anymore about could I. Daggone it! I *was*.

Arriving in just enough time to meet my folks and my sister at the hospital, I knocked on the door and said, "Alright. We're ready for the good news."

My dad bit his lip and nodded his head in agreement. I mean it was good news. If he wasn't going to be with us any longer, he would be with God. And was that bad? If God decided to take him, He'd make us strong enough to be okay with it.

"Well, young man," the doctor said, "you must have been reading my notes and doing some heavy praying 'cause your dad's going to be just fine. He's going to have to take it easy and get more treatments for a while longer but everything looks good. We see no traces of any new tumors."

I went over and hugged my father. "God knew I needed you a while longer."

"No, son. You got the key to this world. He's giving me some more days here so I can be proud of what you have become. You're going to do good things, big things and I'm proud of you."

The two of us welled up with tears. We'd found our purpose and that was to have no purpose other than what God had laid out for us.

It was the weekend of the big ACC track championship. Savoy was on course to set records and be able to compete in some national track and field summer Olympic Games. My girl was bad when it came to the hurdles and 100-meter dash. And though she was the second fastest, a couple months ago she just started smoking everybody. I couldn't believe that my cousin Pillar and Saxon were still hanging in there as a couple. I didn't know how long they would last and I wasn't trying to be in their business, but I hoped that they would stiff it out for a while. They were both in the stands to support my girl.

There was actually a large crowd there. Mr. and Mrs. Lee were there. My folks were there, since they would be helping me move back home for a few weeks until summer classes started. Deuce and Lance were there as well. They were all talking to me at different times and my head was moving from one conversation to the other when I happened to notice Savoy sitting down. Not with the rest of her team, but like she was frustrated. I remembered when I had been at a meet earlier that year and mentally she had messed it up for herself. I needed to give her confidence. I knew what it was like as an athlete to second-guess yourself. But she was a conqueror and she was fierce. She needed to know she was not in this race alone.

When the second event was up and everyone was paying attention to the discus side of the field I jogged down from the stands and said, "Hey! Come here, girl."

"Not right now, Perry. I need to concentrate."

"Come here." Finally she came down the bleachers to where I was.

"I don't think I can do it," she said, looking at me. "This is where it all counts and I'm too nervous to set foot out there."

"You know what? You're speaking negatively, girl." I took my index finger and pointed it to my heart. "I believe in you. God believes in you, too, right in there. Nobody loves this sport like you do. And nobody knows that you haven't even reached the fastest speed you are capable of. So what, you might be hearing negative things. So what, the pressure might be on to do it. Block all that out and go for it. Enjoy this."

"But you don't understand. It's hard."

"Of course I understand. I got sixty- and seventy thousand fans yelling at me during the fall."

"How do you get through it?"

"I block it out. It's just me and God playing. Yeah, I gotta hear what the coaches are saying but whatever. It's like playing the game of life. It's like being in this relationship with you. If it's something you want really bad to work out, you gotta stay focused on this and don't give up. And that's in everything. Your parents are here—they want the best for their daughter. You brother is here and he wants the best for his sister."

"Come on, Perry. Saxon? Can you give me a better example?"

"No, really. He's your biggest fan." I pulled her close and kissed her lips.

"You really think I can do this?"

"Savoy Lee. Woman, as beautiful as you are you can do anything you set your mind to do. You helped me to know that even in my shortcomings I could rise above and do big things. If I can come through you better believe your own words and do the same."

"I just don't want to let everyone down."

"If you fall flat on your face and try your best you won't let any of us down."

"So now you're saying I'm going to fall on my face?" she said in a panicked tone.

"Savoy, calm down! Girl, you know what I mean. Get out there and show off."

"Can you give me another kiss for luck?"

"I'll give you another kiss for love." I kissed her and she jogged back onto the field just in time for her race to begin. She ran the 100-meter dash and before I could blink she was crossing the finish line. The girl might've smoked me, she was just that fast. When she did the hurdles she was phenomenal. A chance to compete for the Olympics track spot would certainly be hers.

Rod, one of the brothers announcing the meet, called out, "Perry Skky Jr. I hear you're in the house. This is the end of the athletic season for Tech. We can't wait for football season. Are you in the house?"

"Man, he ain't here," his brother, D, said.

"He's right here. He's right here."

Of course I had to go down to their table. "What's up, guys?" I slapped their hands.

"Looks like Tech got their ACC championship sewn up. Not only hosting it but they're winning it too. This gives us something to look forward to for football. You got any words for us? You guys gon' be okay? Y'all took it to the National Championship; can you actually win that game this year? Tell us what's up."

"Our team has come a long way this year, you guys. We certainly appreciate the support of all the fans out there. And we believe we're gonna win the National Championship game next year."

"Oh, you got big talk," Rod said. "Why you feel so strongly you can win it?"

"It's not about me. We're a group of collected brothers ready to take on any team we got to face."

"So you guys got a secret weapon?"

"You can say that. A secret weapon to life."

"Share that with us."

"Anyone's life is not about them, personally speaking. When I treat my brother as I would myself I know that there is Someone there looking down on me holding me accountable. When I live with integrity, honesty, joy, and peace in my heart then I can have the right attitude to succeed at anything. So yeah, I think we can be national champs and in so many ways we already are."

Lance came up behind me and started echoing my sentiments. God really was doing something great with us. We were young men, we were football players, but we were His boys. And as long as we kept remembering that, we would be okay. Not doing it alone but step by step, following God in Heaven was the only solution to staying successful and never going astray. Daily following Him and daily finding our way.

A Reading Group Guide

Perry Skky Jr., Book 5:

PROMISE KEPT

Stephanie Perry Moore

ABOUT THIS GUIDE

The following questions are intended to
enhance your group's reading of
PERRY SKKY JR.: PROMISE KEPT
by Stephanie Perry Moore

DISCUSSION QUESTIONS

1. Perry Skky Jr. is trying to please everybody. Is it realistic for him to make promises he can't keep? How do you stand up to the folks you care about and tell them, No?

2. Because of Perry's choice to go to the club with the upperclassmen, he ends up being in the middle of a bar brawl and loses playing time in the biggest game of his life. Do you think he realized he'd let down the team again? If you fall victim to peer pressure and get into trouble, how can you be certain you don't duplicate your lapse in judgment?

3. Because Perry tries to stay out of trouble, another one of his teammates, Saxon, gets ganged up on and ends up fighting for his life. Do you think the way Perry handled the altercation was correct? When things are out of your control and blow up around you, how can you make sure you don't beat yourself up over the outcome?

4. When Perry's grandma dies, after a period of severe grieving he realizes she's in a better place. Do you think Perry can keep his word and try to tell his crew about God? What are some ways you can witness to your friends in a way that they will hear you and not feel like you're being too pushy?

5. When Mario comes and asks Perry for help to get him off drugs, Perry is there. Do you think Perry should have known his old teammate was full of it? How far should you go to be there for a friend on drugs?

6. Perry gets surrounded by the police as he waits for Mario. When the cops pressure him to help them catch

Mario selling drugs, do you think Perry is right to save his own skin and comply? Would you hesitate to rat on a friend that had pulled you into illegal activity?

7. Perry goes on a Spring break trip to unwind with Deuce and Saxon and runs into his sister's friend, who comes on to him. How does Perry try and keep his commitment to God and his girlfriend, Savoy? What are ways you can keep from giving in to temptation?

8. Unfortunately, Perry learns his dad has colon cancer. Do you think Perry is justified in feeling angry with God that his dad has this disease? What price has Jesus paid and does He owe us anything else?

9. Perry and his roommates are shocked when Collin's atheist father wants his son to move out of the apartment with the three Christian guys. Do you think the guys handle the awkward moment correctly? What do you think praying for the unsaved person will do?

10. Perry and Savoy have had one issue after another. Do you think they found a way to be in a healthy relationship and be happy young adults at the end of this series? What things have you learned from reading this series to help you become successful?

Start Your Own Book Club

Courtesy of the PERRY SKKY JR. series

ABOUT THIS GUIDE

The following is intended to help you get
the Book Club you've always wanted
up and running!
Enjoy!

Start Your Own Book Club

A Book Club is not only a great way to make friends, but it is also a fun and safe environment for you to express your views and opinions on everything from fashion to teen pregnancy. A Teen Book Club can also become a forum or venue to air grievances and plan remedies for problems.

The People

To start, all you need is yourself and at least one other person. There's no criteria for who this person or persons should be other than a desire to read and a commitment to read and discuss during a certain time frame.

The Rules

People tend to disagree with each other, cut each other off when speaking, and take criticism personally. So, there should be some ground rules:

1. Do not attack people for their ideas or opinions.
2. When you disagree with a book club member, disagree respectfully. This means that you do not denigrate another person for their ideas. There shouldn't be any name calling or saying, "That's stupid!" Instead, say, "I can respect your position, however, I feel differently."
3. Back up your opinions with concrete evidence, either from the book in question or life in general.
4. Allow everyone a turn to comment.
5. Do not cut a member off when the person is speaking. Respectfully wait your turn.

6. Critique only the idea (and do so responsibly; again, simply saying, "That's stupid!" is not appropriate). Do not criticize the person.
7. Every member must agree to, and abide by, the ground rules.

Feel free to add any other ground rules you think might be necessary.

The Meeting Place

Once you've decided on members and agreed to the ground rules, you should decide on a place to meet. This could be the local library, the school library, your favorite restaurant, a bookstore, or a member's home. Remember, though, if you decide to hold your sessions at a member's home, the location should rotate to another member's home for the next session. It's also polite for guests to bring treats when attending a Book Club meeting at a member's home. If you choose to hold your meetings in a public place, always remember to ask the permission of the librarian or store manager. If you decide to hold your meetings in a local bookstore, ask the manager to post a flyer in the window announcing the Book Club to attract more members if you so desire.

Timing is Everything

Teenagers of today are all much busier than teenagers of the past. You're probably thinking, "Between chorus rehearsals, the Drama Club, and oh yeah, my job, when will I ever have time to read another book that doesn't feature Romeo and Juliet!" Well, there's always time, if it's well-planned and planned ahead. You and your Book Club can decide to meet as often or as little as is appropriate for your bustling schedules. *Once a month* is a favorite option. *Sleepover Book Club* meetings—if you're open to excluding one gender—is also a favorite option. And in this day of high-tech, savvy teens, *Internet Discussion Groups* are also an appealing option. Just choose what's right for you!

Well, you've got the people, the ground rules, the place, and the time. All you need now is a book!

The Book

Choosing a book is the most fun. PROMISE KEPT is of course an excellent choice, and since it's part of a series, you won't soon run out of books to read and discuss. Your Book Club can also have comparative discussions as you compare the first book, PRIME CHOICE, to the second, PRESSING HARD, and so on.

But depending upon your reading appetite, you may want to veer outside of the Perry Skky Jr. series. That's okay. There are plenty of options, many of which you will be able to find under the Dafina Books for Young Readers Program in the coming months.

But don't be afraid to mix it up. Nonfiction is just as good as fiction, and a fun way to learn about from where we came without just using a history textbook. Science fiction and fantasy can be fun, too!

And always research the author. You might find the author has a website where you can post your Book Club's questions or comments. You can correspond with Stephanie Perry Moore by visiting her website, www.stephanieperrymoore.com. She can sit in on your meetings, either in person or on the phone, and this can be a fun way to discuss the book as well!

The Discussion

Every good Book Club discussion starts with questions. PROMISE KEPT, as will every book in the Perry Skky Jr. series, comes along with a Reading Group Guide for your convenience, though of course, it's fine to make up your own. Here are some sample questions to get started:

1. What's this book all about anyway?
2. Who are the characters? Do we like them? Do they remind us of real people?
3. Was the story interesting? Were real issues of concern to you examined?
4. Were there details that didn't quite work for you or ring true?
5. Did the author create a believable environment—one that you could visualize?
6. Was the ending satisfying?
7. Would you read another book from this author?

Record Keeper

It's generally a good idea to have someone keep track of the books you read. Often libraries and schools will hold reading drives where you're rewarded for having read a certain number of books in a certain time period. Perhaps a pizza party awaits!

Get Your Teachers and Parents Involved

Teachers and parents love it when kids get together and read. So involve your teachers and parents. Your Book Club may read a particular book where it would help to have an adult's perspective as part of the discussion. Teachers may also be able to include what you're doing as a Book Club in the classroom curriculum. That way books you love to read such as PROMISE KEPT can find a place in your classroom.

Resources

To find some new favorite writers, check out the following resources. Happy reading!

Young Adult Library Services Association
http://www.ala.org/ala/yalsa/yalsa.htm

Carnegie Library of Pittsburgh
Hip-Hop!
Teen Rap Titles
http://www.carnegielibrary.org/teens/read/booklists/teenrap.html

TeensPoint.org
What Teens Are Reading
http://www.teenspoint.org/reading_matters/book_list.asp?sort=5&list=274

Teenreads.com
http://www.teenreads.com

Sacramento Public Library
Fantasy Reading for Kids
http://www.saclibrary.org/teens/fantasy.html

Book Divas
http://www.bookdivas.com

Meg Cabot Book Club
http://www.megcabotbookclub.com

Stay tuned for the new series by
Stephanie Perry Moore, "Beta Gamma Pi,"
available Spring 2009 wherever books are sold.
College pledging has never been so juicy,
so don't miss the first novel in the new series.

Catch up with Perry Skky Jr. from the beginning
with PRIME CHOICE, Book 1 in the Perry Skky Jr. series
available now wherever books are sold!

~ 1 ~

Needing a Yes

"Come on, Tori, you know this feels good. Just say yes," I said as I kissed my girlfriend of two years on the ear.

When she pulled away, it ticked me off worse than I could describe. Why'd she lead me on? I had committed to dating only her for the past two years and now that we were into the third, it was time for her to put up or, dag, I'd have to move on.

"You're mad," she said as she bit her pretty fingernails.

The stare I gave her was cold. There was no need to answer her question. I had just gone from really wanting to be with her to wanting our relationship to be over. I mean, I didn't have time to play games. This is my senior year. I was a highly recruited wide receiver. The schools in the Atlantic Coast Conference and the South Eastern Conference wanted me badly. Every time I stepped into a party, girls were lining up to get with me. And here I was, trying to do the right thing. Wanting to be faithful to one girl. All for nothing.

Before I could make it to the door, Tori pulled me back into her arms.

"Perry, don't walk out like this. I love you. I'm just not ready. I know this is your last year in high school and all, but I'm not ready for sex. You used to understand that. Why are you changing all of a sudden?"

I shrugged. "I got different needs now. I can't explain it. I just don't know. I'm tired of this game, Tori. I want your actions to speak louder than your words."

I went and sat back down on the couch and put my head down on my knees and tried to cool off. The girl needed to let me leave. She wasn't ready to do nothing. Maybe our relationship had gone as far as it could go.

I believed in God, but I wasn't really completely walking with the Lord. I was baptized in the sixth grade and felt that God and I had an understanding. Though He wanted me to remain pure until marriage, I believed He would be straight with the fact that I wasn't trying to sleep around like my crazy boys.

I wanted my first time to be with a girl I deeply cared for. I only wanted the best for Tori. I didn't want anybody to mess with her. I liked protecting her and having her around. Yeah, Tori Guice was the one I wanted to take things to the next level with, but she wouldn't let me. I lifted up my head when I felt her stroking the back of my neck.

Even physically I had changed a lot in the last year. My body had stretched from 6 feet 1 inch to 6 feet 3 inches. Everybody kept hollering at me, askin' when would I play hoops. But football was my thing. The extra height would be a plus to the new season, with me trying to impress all the college coaches. There wasn't too many defenders, corner backs or defensive backs that would be able to cover me on the field. I knew my extra height would give me an advantage to catch balls thrown high with my name on them. Even the track coach was on me to run in the off season.

Every aspect of my life was cool except this one. My older sister, Payton, would be out of my hair away at college in a bit. Actually, I liked her a lot more now than I did when she used to take up the bathroom space. She had much drama her senior year and I wasn't going there. My grades were good. I had five college visits set up in the next three months and had turned down five more. My dad had hooked me up with a two-door sports ride from his dealership. Life was on the up for the most part.

Yeah, Tori was a cutie and I wanted to stay with her, but she wasn't going to mess up my flow. *Now what was she doing?* I thought. She knew better than to stroke my head like that. She was making a brotha feel things that made my heart race fast. I turned toward her and kissed her passionately til she pulled away from me again.

"Perry, I thought you liked me for *me*. I thought you were okay with the fact that I didn't want to go all the way," she said as she fastened her pants I'd worked hard to unloose.

"Obviously you don't understand," I said to her as I got up. "I'm tired of being the bad guy for wanting my girlfriend to make me feel good. You know I'm a good guy. I don't mistreat you and I've never cheated on you. Reward me!"

I had been at her house for two hours and I had only intended to be there for about an hour 'cause we knew her dad would walk through the door at six. Now it was after six. And there Mr. Guice was—standing tall.

He squinted his eyes and surveyed the room. "Perry, I thought you were only supposed to drop my daughter off. Tori, is your mom home?"

I knew I was thrown up under the bus at that point (a saying my dad always used when trouble came his way). Maybe God was up there watching out for me. I couldn't imagine being caught in the position I wanted us to be in. Mr. Guice would have had my head for sure.

I walked toward the door. "Hey, sir, sorry, sorry. I gotta go."

"Nah, man, wait. Let's talk about the upcoming football season. My daughter stressing you out?" he asked as he gave Tori a disappointed smirk.

It was always funny to me how fathers tolerated a little extra when their daughter was dating a guy they respected. I watched my dad do that with Payton's boyfriends, Dakari and Tad. Now Mr. Guice was playing that stuff with me. I mean, really, what did he think we were in here arguing about? Our clothes were on, but they weren't straight.

"Oh, Dad, you think it's my fault? Well, how's this? Your hero Perry Skky Jr. wants to have sex with me. Should I do that to keep him happy?" Upset, Tori walked right past her father and went outside.

Mr. Guice leaned so close up to me I could feel the fire in his heart. "Is what my daughter said true, son? I don't mind y'all having a kiss here and a hug sometimes, but we had an understanding. You promised me no lines would be crossed. You changing the rules on me?"

Boy, I didn't want to lie to that man. However, there was no way that I could tell him that some nights all I could think about was his daughter's chest, lips and thighs. I was raised in a good home. My folks taught me to be a cool kid but have respect for my elders. I wasn't a punk, but I wasn't a thug, either. My boys ragged me for not having sex sometimes, but I held my own so they knew not to take jokes too far. Actually, I think they appreciated my stance. How was I to answer Tori's dad?

"What's up? You can't even be man enough to tell me that you wanna take my daughter's innocence away?" he asked as I stood frozen before him. "I know. I remember what high school was like. So listen here, partner: I'm gonna let you walk out my house with all your faculties intact 'cause you gonna do one of two things—remember the rules of this game or play with another girl. Are we clear?"

"Yes, sir."

"Now, you go out there and tell my daughter to get her tail back in here, talking smart to me like she done lost her mind. I gotta set her straight, too."

"All right, sir."

I grabbed my keys and headed out the door. I had every

intent of getting in my car, pumping up the music and cruising on home. I couldn't find Tori, though. When I did, she was in her backyard under the gazebo, crying. I cared too much for her to just stroll away.

When I sat down beside her and touched her hand, her eyes were closed but she knew it was me. As she fell into my arms, a part of me wanted to forget everything I wanted and stop wanting more. But was that realistic?

I prayed to God: "*Lord, this is hard. As I smell my girlfriend's sweet perfume, I want something from her that You tell me I shouldn't have now. I'm struggling and really need You to help me keep my feelings checked.*"

"Perry, I'm sorry," she said, still sobbing. "I do wanna be with you. I know you could have anybody at our school and you want me. Ciara and Briana tell me all the time how I need to just put out."

"Listen to me, Tori," I said as I lifted her up off my shoulder. "I only want you if you want me. It ain't right for me to force you into doing it my way, and you shouldn't let your girls dish you into doing it the way they do, 'cause, trust me, my boys Damarius and Cole don't deserve them."

Tori laughed with tears still flowing. She knew how true that was. They were players and though I didn't agree with them being untrue to their girls, I couldn't stop them. That's why I guess I was so mad that Tori wasn't ready for us to go further. I wasn't planning to do her like that. Even though I wanted her in my life, we were at a gridlock. I had to end this.

Kissing her on the forehead, I said, "Tori, I don't want to hurt you. You know you got my heart, but we want something different. I got to let this go for now, you and me."

"No, Perry, no! Please don't do that."

As if she wasn't already crying hard enough, she flipped out in a way I'd never seen. But I had never broken up with her before. Even though I was moved, I realized something had a hold on her that was making her not take it to the next level with me. I knew it was her Christian beliefs. How could I mess with that? I was struggling with letting God down myself. I had to leave her alone even though it was killing me to see her so sad.

"You'll always be special to me, though, Tori. Your dad wants you inside. Call me." Then I squeezed her hands, left the gazebo and drove away.

I wasn't in my room for five minutes when my crazy sister opened up the door without knocking.

"Hey, little brother. What's up?" she asked, too bubbly for me.

Payton had a couple more weeks before she went back to school at the University of Georgia. She and I had done a lot of fun stuff over the summer. We went white-water rafting on our family trip to California. We spent time sightseeing in DC. I actually enjoyed the Broadway play we saw in New York. My sister was the bomb, but at that moment I needed my space.

"Oh, so you don't wanna talk to me," she said, being her naturally obtrusive self. "I know when you shut your door somethin' ain't right."

"What you talking about?"

"Who's done something to you?"

"If you gotta know, I cut Tori off."

"Oh, I know what this is about. So it's like that," my sister said as she stood near my bed. "You think you're ready?"

"Guess so."

"Then I'm so glad Tori stood her ground. I'm going to just let you sit here and sulk about the mistake you just made."

As Payton shut my door, I knew she was right. I was already regretting my decision, but it was done and I was going to stand by it. I didn't need to be tied down, no way. This was my senior year and I was going to get *mine*. The Lord just needed to help me find out what *mine* really was.

Catch up with Perry Skky Jr. from the beginning
with PRESSING HARD, Book 2 in the Perry Skky Jr. series
available now wherever books are sold!

~ 1 ~

Grooving too Much

"You a punk. A little mama's boy. That's why you won't have a drink," Damarius taunted as I helped him carry beer from the car to his house for the New Year's Eve jam he was about to host.

I was tired of it. He could call me whatever he wanted to. Say whatever he wanted to say. I didn't care. He wasn't going to pressure me into doing something I wasn't ready to do.

"Come on, Cole," Damarius said, looking to our friend for back up. "You need to admit it too. That's what you think of his tail. Do you think he all that? He hadn't never even had a piece, drank a little nip or smoked a joint. Dang! Perry ain't no real man yet."

I wanted to take one of those six packs and bust him across the head with it. But because we were late setting things up, I let it go. As we entered the house, Cole spoke up.

"All right you two. Kiss and make up," he said before Damarius and I went our separate ways.

It didn't take the place long to fill up. Not only were there a lot of kids from my school in the house, but folks from all over Augusta were showing up. I felt sort of bad that I didn't call my girl, Savoy, but honestly the whole commitment thing was scaring me a bit. I didn't want to feel pressured into a relationship with her. I hadn't seen her since Christmas night, but I thought about her all the time.

As I walked around scanning the crowd, I thought about Damarius accusing me of being a punk. So if a brother didn't get high or get wasted, then he wasn't cool? I knew Damarius was just jealous. I didn't need anything to make me feel good about me. I was high off of life. College coaches were always trying to persuade me to change my choice from going to Georgia Tech. Girls always trying to get with me. Brothers always wanting me to attend their functions or just to hang out with them to raise their stock with the ladies. I had it like that.

At that moment, none of that meant a thing to me. I wanted respect from my boy. Was proving to him that I could handle alcohol the only way I could get him off my back? I don't know why I was letting him get to me. Maybe I should just pray about it. After all, I had learned this year that if I just give it to God, He'd make my situation better.

Deep down I had to admit that I felt as if I was at the sidelines looking on. I peered in like I was watching this stuff on the TV or something. Maybe I had issues and I needed to release, let go, and get down.

When I stepped into the hallway, I saw Jaboe, a thug from down the block. Jaboe was a high school dropout who should have graduated with my sister's class two years ago, but he started selling drugs. He told the world that he could make way more money hustling than he ever could the legitimate way.

"Hey man. I'm good for it! You ain't gotta jack me up like that," Damarius told Jaboe as the thug grabbed him by his collar and squeezed it tight.

What did my boy get himself into? It was hard for me to believe that he was doing drugs. The pressure of wanting to get into a major college had given my buddy a new perspective on right from wrong.

"I want some bills, boy. I don't want no change," Jaboe said as he slung the coins in his hand to the floor. "You got all these folks in here for free. You better start charging some money next time you have a party 'cause I want my paper. If I don't get it next week, not only will you be cut off from the stash," he said as he took a knife out of his pocket and put it to Damarius's face, "but you know what else is next."

Damarius tried talking his way out of the problem. "All right, dude. Ease up! I'm gonna get yo' money. Give me a little credit. You know I'm good for it."

I had no idea that my boy was smoking more than cigarettes. No wonder his grades were slipping.

Regardless of how he felt about me, I had to stop him from messing his life up. Like Reverend McClep preached at church last Sunday, I was my brother's keeper. I wasn't going to let Damarius go down like that. I saw Jaboe pull out a dime bag and I quickly intercepted it, as if I was a defensive back on the field or something and tossed it back up in his face. "He doesn't want that," I said to Jaboe.

I looked over his shoulder at the two guys with him. One had cornrows with even parts going down to the back of his head and a grill, and the other dude was thicker than Mr. T himself. They stepped toward me, but I wasn't backing down. I didn't care how long Damarius had been messing around with that stuff. It was going to end today.

"Come on, Perry. What's up? You crazy? This is business," Damarius said to me.

"Is there a problem?" Jaboe asked, his eyes threatening.

"No, man, there ain't no problem," Damarius said, stepping between us.

"Like D said, no problem. He just don't need your stuff. So thanks for coming," I said, pointing to the front door.

"What's up, Damarius? You gonna let him talk for you? Or a betta question, you gonna let him talk to me like that?" Jaboe pulled up his sweater and showed us he was packing.

Throwing my hands up, I said, "I don't mean no disrespect Jaboe. Look, he just don't need it, all right?"

"Yeah, I hear you." He laughed and dropped his top, concealing the weapon again. "Cool, I ain't trying to push my stuff off on anybody, but I do want my money."

"You'll get it. Soon, man," Damarius promised.

Jaboe and his gangster boys left. Damarius tried to go off on me about the whole thing.

Getting in my face, he said, "Man! What's up? Are you crazy? You'll mess up your whole life getting in Jaboe's way."

I couldn't believe he tried to play me instead of thank me. "You need to pay him the little money you owe him and leave him alone before you end up like him, on the corner somewhere. He's reduced to hiding out from the cops and bullying folks into giving him dollars."

"You don't know what you just did, Perry. Stay out of my business," he said, shaking his head as he walked past me to join the crowd in the living room. I was just about to leave the party when I heard Damarius announce over the DJ's system, "Hey y'all! Hey y'all! Y'all know my boy Perry here don't drink, right?"

What he was doing? Why was he calling me out like that?

"But it's New Year's Eve, and we want him to have a little fun, right y'all?" The crowd started chanting, "Yeaaa, Perry! Drink! Drink! Drink!"

I went over to him and whispered, "What's up with this?"

"You all up in my business! You can't knock what I enjoy until you try it. Was I right earlier, Perry? Are you a punk?"

Without even thinking, I took the beer out of his hand, twisted off the top, and gulped it down. I didn't even have time to decide if I liked the taste or not. A random guy from the crowd ran up to me with another one. I wasn't no punk. Damarius was not about to play me like that. I twisted off the cap and chugged that one down, too.

"Drink! Drink! Drink! Drink!" folks called out.

"Can you handle one more, big boy?" Damarius dared.

Cole came up and said, "Man, that's enough. What you trying to do to him, D?"

"I can handle it. I'll show you it ain't all that. Give me another one." All I could hear was more chanting from the crowd when I drank the next brew.

After a few minutes I was feeling a little light-headed. But it was all good. Someone handed me another one with the top already off. I couldn't tell if someone had drunk out of it or not, but it really didn't matter. I drank it down, and when I was done, the crowd yelled and screamed louder than fans did at any football game I'd ever played in. I was feeding off of it. A couple of girls came up to me and got close: one in the front and one in the back. They swayed their hips from left to right, and my hips started moving too. Oh, the party was on.

Damarius came up to me. "Dang, man. You can hold your stuff. All right. All right. My bad." He laughed and walked away.

After a couple of dances, I went up to the DJ and started trying to spin records, which I have no skills with at all on a regular day. But being a little intoxicated, nobody could tell me that I wasn't the life of the party. The sad thing was that I couldn't go anywhere without the two girls, Q and Jo, following me. It was cute, but I was getting tired of them.

"You know what? Y'all gotta give a brother some space. Dang, I can't even dance with nobody else."

They looked as if I had hurt their feelings.

"I'm sorry. I'm just being honest."

"You all right, boy?" Damarius said as he came over to me and handed me another beer. "I thought you wanted this. I didn't want you to have to look for it."

Cole grabbed it out of my hand. "No, no, D. He done had enough for real."

"Whatcha mean, I done had enough?"

"Tell 'em. Perry, tell 'em. You feeling good right about now, right?" Damarius said.

"Good? I feel the same. Whatcha talking about?"

I was so out of it, I didn't even know what Damarius was talking about.

"Naw, Perry," Cole said, turning away.

"Man, give me that beer!" I grabbed the beer out of my boy's hand, spilling some of it on the floor. Sipping the beer, I stepped around my boys so I could get back to dancing.

I stopped and had to blink my eyes a couple of times when I saw my ex, Tori, standing in the middle of a crowd. She still looked as fine as she always did. Her hair was all done up, her nails were manicured just right, and she was wearing this cute little pink number that hugged her body just right.

"What's up girl? Dang. A brother can't get no love."

She yanked my hand and pulled me down the hall. She pushed me into Damarius's bedroom and shut the door.

"Uhh-ha. What's up? You wanna give yourself to me now? I just asked for a hug. I didn't know you wanted to give it up."

"Perry, I love you too much to see you act like this. What's going on?"

"What you talking about? Dang! You pulled me up in here. I don't need no girl giving me a hard time by telling me what to do. We don't go together no more, and I guess I should be glad of that."

"You making a fool of yourself tonight, okay."

"Man, I'm the life of this joint."

"No, people are staring at you because you are tripping over yourself. Drool is coming out of your mouth. It's clear you can't hold alcohol."

"Girl, shut up. Leave me alone. Bye. Get out. I'm sorry I asked for some love. I got another girl, dang. She's prettier than you."

The moment I said that, I wanted to take my words back, but I knew that wasn't possible because Tori had heard me. She looked devastated. I felt bad. I didn't mean to hurt her, but the alcohol was speaking.

"You got somebody else?"

"Forget it. Forget it. I just need to be alone."

"I mean, you just said it! You said you got somebody else! Talk to me! Tell me! Is it somebody at our school? Is it somebody I know? We haven't been broke up but a couple of months, and you already got another girlfriend?"

"I ain't said I had another girlfriend. Dang. Y'all females be tripping."

"I'm not tripping. I should have expected it. I mean, everywhere I go, girls are telling me I'm stupid for letting you go and not giving it up. If they not telling me that, they telling me they plan to satisfy you. So hey, I'm not surprised. I might as well have a drink with you," she said as she came over, trying to get what was left in my bottle.

"Go on now. You don't need this. Seriously. Look, look!" I said as I shoved her to the side.

I didn't mean to push her, but again, I didn't have complete control of my faculties. What was supposed to be just a little push moved her halfway across the room towards the door.

"Okay. Fine. I get it. You don't have to hurt me worse than you already have, okay." She opened the door and dashed out.

After she left, I stood staring at the open door, upset and confused. I realized what I had done, and I wanted to go after her, but I began to feel a terrible burning sensation in my chest. What was going on?

I couldn't understand why I was having such horrible physical pain. It was like I was having a heart attack or something. I couldn't even make it to Damarius's bed. I fell straight to the floor. I couldn't breathe. I felt like I was going to die.

The only thing I could do was pray: *Lord, I'm sorry. You gotta help me, though. I was stupid to drink. Being pressured and all. Yeah, I gotta admit it felt good for a minute, but right now, I feel worse than as if three linebackers tackled me. Please Lord, please.*

I couldn't even pray anymore. I looked up at Damarius's light, which was circling around and around in his room, thinking about all the hopes and dreams I had for myself. I wondered if this was going to be the end. Stupidity might have done me in. Maybe Tori was right about me thinking I was cool. I had not only hurt her feelings, but also I'd probably made a complete idiot out of myself. All of a sudden, I heard the door open. I didn't know who it was, but I certainly didn't want anyone to see me unable to keep my composure. But there was nothing I could do about that now.

"Perry, man, what's up? What's up?" Cole yelled as he rushed to my side.

"I don't feel good, man." I was so happy to see him.

"See. I told Damarius you didn't need all that beer."

"Man, what am I suppose to do? My chest is burning for real."

"You gotta take deep breaths."

"You ever felt like this?"

"I gotta get you some water."

"Water? That's gonna help?"

"I'll be right back. Just hold on."

My boy left and it seemed like it was taking him forever to come back. *Why did teenagers drink?* I started asking myself. At first I could feel it. There was some pleasure in it. It made me feel good, confident, and larger than life. Now here I was, helpless. When I heard the door open again, I yelled, "Call the ambulance."

"See, I told you he was hurting," Cole said to Damarius.

"He'll be all right. Just give him the doggone water. Boy, you can't hold nothing."

I drank the water and took deep breaths as they helped me onto Damarius's bed.

"You just need to rest and relax."

"I still don't feel good y'all, for real."

"Dang! I gotta bring the party in here. Nobody gonna believe this. He can't hold his own."

I didn't even care at that moment. But I heard Cole taking up for me.

I lay in that bed for the next five minutes, vowing to the Lord that I would never ever go over the top with alcohol again if I survived this situation. I thought about my parents, and how this would let them down. They had raised me better than that, even though all my life I had been pushed by my peers to do stuff. I'd always been the leader, applying positive peer pressure. But here I was caught up in the wrong mess. I was trying to keep Damarius from smoking his brains away, and he turns around and pushes me to put something I don't need into my body. I now knew none of this was worth it. Trying to impress people. Trying to be in the in-crowd. All that stuff was silly. I had to stay in my lane and run my race. As I took a deep breath and watched my chest rise higher and higher, I hated that I was grooving too much.

Catch up with Perry Skky Jr. from the beginning
with PROBLEM SOLVED, Book 3 in the Perry Skky Jr. series
available now wherever books are sold!

~ 1 ~

Understanding the Difference

Now, I know better. When a white person looks at me, they either see a rising football star or just another hoodlum. I didn't get the latter look often because I was known for my moves on the field. I guess I was sheltered. I didn't have much interaction with people of a different culture or race. So when Saxon and I stood at the steel hotel doorway of our introduction to society Beautillion party that was getting a bit out of control, and the manager stood in front of both of us looking like he wanted to grab us by the necks and throw us in jail, I didn't know how to take it. Racism was hitting me straight in the face. No part of me liked that.

But Saxon seemed familiar with the disturbing actions of the man. He took the lead and said, "Alright, man, we hear you. We're just having a little fun. Dang. We pay our money just like everybody else. You just trying to get on us 'cause we're black."

"Now, son, there's no need to toss the race card around," the red-faced manager said, looking away.

"Wait, hold up," Saxon said as he stepped up into the man's beaming red face. "I am not your son."

"Okay, you need to step back then," the manager asked, realizing he wasn't dealing with a punk.

Saxon and I had never been cool. Truthfully, we both had egos. We were both *the man* at our respective schools. It was going to be interesting playing ball with him at Georgia Tech in the next couple of months. He was a wild guy and I didn't have much respect for the dude. However, my life hadn't been perfect either. So in some ways we were cut from the same piece of sirloin. And I felt a bond with him when the manager tried him.

Though there wasn't alcohol in the room where the party was jumping off, I wasn't a fool. I could smell Saxon had been tipping in someone's jar. The last thing he needed was to be hauled off for letting his mouth get the best of him. So I pushed him back into the room with the rest of the folks.

I said to the riled-up guy, "I got this boy. Get in there."

Over my shoulder Saxon said, "Tell me something then. Because you'd better talk some sense into him. Shoot, I'm about to bust a—"

"Man, go," I said, grabbing the doorknob and trying to shut Saxon inside. "Sir, I'm sorry for my friend."

"You don't need to apologize for me," Saxon said as the door closed.

I looked over at the manager and said, "Really, sir, we'll keep it down."

The manager nodded in approval of my words. "I'm just saying, young man, this is a respectable hotel. We didn't mind having your event in the ballroom, but we don't allow room parties, and if you can assure me that you people will keep it down, then I won't bother you."

Again this man was ticking me off. *You people*. What in the heck did he mean by that? I guess he saw fire in my eyes. He backed away.

"Well, I'll leave you to your guest now," the manager said.

I closed the door in anger. Saxon came up to me. His breath was stronger than before.

"Want a little," he said, holding out a bottle of gin.

"Naw, man, I'm straight," I said to him as I looked around the place for his gorgeous sister.

Saxon followed me. "See, wh . . . white men think they can talk to the black man any kinda way. My dad gets that crap all the time on his job, but I won't ever let someone think they can handle me without dis . . . spect."

"You mean respect, Sax," I said, trying to keep up with what he was saying.

"Whatever, man, you know what I'm saying. You feel me, too. I saw the heated look on your face when you came back in here. He said something that ticked you off, right?"

I didn't respond. Saxon grabbed my shirt. He shook me.

"Let's go jack him up. We need to teach him a lesson," the drunk boy said.

Taking his paws off me, I said, "Boy, go party. We both need to cool down."

Then I stopped his sister. I couldn't go get with her, though, because she was dancing with some other dude. But as I watched him rub his hands up her fine thighs, I knew I had to let her know how I felt.

However, someone was banging on the door from the outside. My first thought was that the manager had come back too soon. And if it was him, maybe Saxon's idea wasn't such a crazy one after all.

Opening the wooden door, frustrated, I said, "What?"

"Boy, you can't yell at that pretty lady," Saxon said over my shoulder at the sight of my sister. "Come in, come in."

"Sax, get back," I said as he tried to grab her butt. "Your cousin will get you, man, and my dad will, too."

"Oh, Payton, dang, that's Tad's girl? Payton, you look different," Saxon said. "I didn't mean no harm."

"We're cool, Sax," Payton said to him.

"What's up?" I asked her.

She said, "Mom and Dad are in their room on the floor below and want to see you. Folks have been complaining about the noise, Perry."

If I wasn't mad enough already, I was really boiling then. We were just teens having fun. Shucks, the music wasn't that loud.

"You staying or what?" I asked my sister.

"Naw, Tad is coming after he gets off and I gave him Mom's room number."

Shutting the door as we entered the hall, I said sarcastically, "That was smart."

She hit me. Though Payton was kidding, I clammed up. We walked to the elevator in silence.

"What's up with you? I was just joking," she asked as she pushed the button for our parents' floor once we got on.

"Not you, sis," I said as we got off the elevator. "I'm just tired that's all. And I don't want Dad going off on me tonight. I'm not in the mood."

My dad opened the door as if he was waiting for me to arrive. "Junior, I can hear you guys."

I heard noise as well, but the bass beat sounded off. I figured I didn't need to argue with him. I'd let him speak his peace and then I'd be on my way.

"Look, you asked for your own room and I agreed to pay for it. Don't make me regret that decision. The hotel manager called me and said he's been getting complaints about the noise. I knew you were going to have some of your friends over, but boy, don't y'all tear up nothing. And kids can't be drinking in there. Be responsible."

"Dad, I got it," I let out before turning to head back.

"Junior, I'm not finished talking to you."

Sighing and facing him again, I said, "What else, Dad?"

"Look, son, I'm not trying to spoil the party. If that was the case, I would have come down there myself. Just know the rules are different for black kids. Some white folks only tolerate so much. So don't give them a reason to shut your fun down, understand?" he asked.

"Got it."

He said, "Now, Payton, go with him and make sure things stay in line."

"But Dad, Tad's coming here," my sister said.

"Good, he and I need to have a little chat and then I'll send him your way. I don't want y'all too close." He shut the door on both of us.

My sister vented. "Ugh!"

She took the word right out my mouth. We looked at the elevator and saw a lot of people were waiting for it. Payton suggested we take the stairs up one flight. I agreed. When we got around the corner, awfully loud rock music was coming from a room. I peered inside and saw tons of white kids jamming. Then it hit me. What my father was hearing was from around the corner, not from above.

This blond-headed dude came out into the hall. "Hey, y'all are welcome to come in."

"Naw, man, we're straight," I said to him, "But tell me something, are you getting any complaints on the noise from the hotel?"

"Complaints, naw, dude." He looked at my sister and smiled like he wanted her.

"That's my sister, but she's taken," I leaned in and said to him before quickly realizing he was just as drunk as Saxon.

"Cool, man, y'all come back," he said.

Payton and I both laughed and we headed to our jam. When we arrived, the hotel manager was walking back toward our door. I wanted him to ask me to keep things quiet.

"Mr. Skky, the noise seems to be growing from this room. I'm afraid I need you to ask your guests to leave. You understand?"

I laughed. "Sir, we just left the party down below us and they have their speakers blasting louder than ours. And since you're not asking them to curtail their fun, maybe you'd better look the other way on our fun as well. Not unless you want me to report this to your superiors? Are you understanding me?"

"Oh well, Mr. Skky, no need to get upset. Just keep the noise down as best you can. Sorry I bothered you." The manager turned and walked away.

I was glad I had caught him being unfair. However, I was saddened to know things like that happen to black kids. But at least it felt good fighting injustice the right way and winning.

Getting back on the floor where the party was, Payton was excited to see her boyfriend standing out front of the door.

"Hey, baby!" she ran up to him and said.

I didn't have any problems with it. Though I was her little brother, I was very protective of my sister. However, I liked Tad, too. He was a good guy. I actually sort of admired a lot of his ways. He was a strong believer in God and I know I wasn't there yet, but I was certainly striving to hopefully have that kind of relationship with God myself.

"Where y'all been? Your father told me you were up here. I have been waiting up here for a bit," he said to the both of us after they let go of their embrace.

"Nothing, my brother just stopped off at another party."

"Dang, y'all been party-hopping without me? Nobody coming on to my girl, are they?"

I looked at Payton and she at me. I knew she didn't want me to say anything. She was hot and Tad knew it.

"Oh, so somebody was!" he exclaimed, and I could see that he valued my sister.

She opened the door, ignoring him, and walked inside. The place was more packed than we had left it, and some of the people I saw in the small cramped room weren't even at the ball, but when there was a party, I shouldn't have been surprised that it could draw folks from everywhere.

I frantically scanned the room looking for Savoy, but I couldn't find her. I hoped that she hadn't left. Even though I had apologized for messing up our relationship, somehow I felt I still needed to explain that I cared.

"Oh, so what's up? You looking for my cousin, huh?" Tad said to me.

Tad and I were cool. I think he liked me a little bit better than he liked his first cousin Saxon, Savoy's brother. And that is probably because I had some type of morals. I wasn't all the way on the Holy Holy side of the scale, but I certainly wasn't slumming in the gutters with Satan like Saxon either. But I had done his cousin wrong and I didn't know how he'd feel about that. Shucks, I didn't even know if he knew what had gone down between the two of us.

"Oh, so what, you can't talk to me? I know you looking for Savoy. And I know what went down between the two of y'all," he said.

Though I knew he could be understanding, I mean Tad was even practicing abstinence—my sister was having a hard time keeping her loins under control. If it wasn't for Tad leading the Lord's way, they would have fallen a long time ago.

"Man, look, I'm not perfect so don't think that I am," Tad surprised me by saying. "I want to get with your sister so bad, but you know I just ask the Lord to keep me wanting to please Him more than I want to please my own flesh and so far that has helped. Everybody makes mistakes; my cousin isn't perfect either. You guys are about to go to college so there is no reason why . . . If you want to talk to her, be real with her. Y'all can work something out."

"You think she'll listen?" I finally opened up to him and asked.

"I don't know, there she is over there," he said, pointing to the girl I couldn't find. "Why don't you go ask her?"

I nodded and headed over in her direction.

She wasn't smiling and she wasn't walking toward me. Thankfully she wasn't walking away.

"Hey!" I said nonchalantly when I got right upon her face.

She replied, "Hey."

"Wanna dance?"

"I've been dancing all night, I'm a little tired of dancing," she said.

"You want to step outside in the hall and talk? We can walk around the hotel."

"Yeah, we can do that," she said.

I was so excited to have a bit of her time. I mean, I didn't deserve it. We said we were going to be in a committed relationship and I broke that vow not even more than a month after we made it. How could she ever trust me again? But when I looked into her gorgeous dark brown eyes, I knew I had to try. It messed with me a bit to see her in someone else's arms. And although it was all my fault, if there was anything I could do to reverse it, I had to try.

"So what did you want to talk about?" she asked when we got outside by the pool.

Being a popular guy, I could tell when girls wanted to get with me. They would wink, laugh at nothing, or stand real close to me; wear revealing clothes and sometimes even give me their underwear. But Savoy's distant stance was far from inviting. Again she asked with her arms folded, "What did you want to talk about?"

I didn't know how to begin so I looked away. Then she replied, "You know what? Maybe this wasn't a good idea, the two of us being alone up under the moon, stars, and all. I can't do this, Perry."

Before she walked away, I grabbed her hand. "I messed up. I told you I messed up. Wait, Savoy, don't leave!"

"Why should I stay?" she asked.

"Because you have to know how I feel."

She chuckled. "Come on, Perry, your actions told me how you feel about me. I'm not angry with you, I told you that, but you can't expect me to forget that it happened."

"No, no. I know you can't forget, but I don't want you to dwell on it."

"Yeah, right!" she said, stepping away from me. "There are some nights I can't even sleep because all I can do is imagine you in Tori's arms."

"Okay, maybe we can't be boyfriend-girlfriend anymore, maybe that was too strong of a title for us anyway, but can't we just hang out—do this thing, see where it takes us?"

"Why should I reinvest time in something that I tried and didn't work out?"

As she was talking, I didn't hear what she was saying. All I could see was her juicy lips asking me to kiss them. So I did. At first she was resistant, pushing me back a little, but her lips never left mine. And then she melted some, didn't give me so much turmoil, and then I knew what I felt for her she felt for me as well. We weren't headed to the altar or anything, but in that kiss, in that moment, in that embrace, I knew we weren't through. And when we pulled away, Savoy knew it, too.

"I guess us spending time together in the end isn't going to hurt anybody, but I am ready to go back to the party now. Perry, I mean—we can't do this! Kissing me and all, why are you trying to confuse me? You cheated on me, okay?"

"I was wrong and stupid, I'm sorry! Can't you see I feel something for you?"

"Yeah, and that's what worries me, because maybe what you're feeling is something that could get us both into trouble, and we'll both end up regretting our actions like you say you are regretting yours and Tori's. I don't know, maybe it's not a good idea for the both of us to hang out. I gotta go back now."

She didn't even wait for me to catch up to her as she opened the back door of the hotel and walked through the ballroom corridor. I wanted to reach out and pull her close to me, but I had to realize that it just wasn't the place where the two of us were anymore and it was my fault. When the elevator door opened, she had her hand on her hip and her mouth looked pissed.

I got in, then she said, "You know what? I'm just going to take the stairs. I'll see you up there."

"I can walk with you," I said.

"Nah."

She let the elevator doors shut with me inside. Alone. Or I thought I was alone. The white dude from the party earlier was behind me, squatting in the corner on the floor.

"Dang, man, that must be your girl. She looks mad, dude. What did you do?"

Even though the beer had him talking sluggishly, his relationship senses were keenly awake.

"Man, you black boys are dumb. There's no way I'd let a girl with a butt looking that good get away from me." He went to press the elevator buttons. "Open up the door. I want to go talk to her."

"Awh naw, partna, mmm-mmm, you stay back," I said as I grabbed his arm and took it away from the buttons.

"That's where I know you . . . you're that state football dude that plays all good and going to Tech and all. I'm a Bulldog, man!"

"I hear yah, partna."

"Well, let me just say this: I always heard that black boys

have a lot of pride. And that might be fine, but that's why you're in this here elevator with me instead of with that girl."

When the elevator opened again, it was his floor. He said, "You better lay down your pride and think about what I'm saying and go after what you want, you understand?"

I never caught his name. He was cool and he was drunk, but he had a point. Savoy wasn't going to make it easy for me to get back in her good graces, and maybe that made me like her more.

Catch up with Perry Skky Jr. from the beginning with PRAYED UP, Book 4 in the Perry Skky Jr. series available now wherever books are sold!

~ 1 ~

Going Over It

"Aw, Perry, please. Be for real. Of all four of us, you are the one with the least past drama. You are a goody-goody," Lance Shadrach said, as Deuce Avery and Collin Cox, my other two college roommates, laughed along with him.

It wasn't like the three of them were getting under my skin or anything, but I did sort of feel a need to defend myself. To most on the outside looking in, I had it going on. I had a physical body that most would kill for, and I now stood six feet four and a half inches tall. Weighing a thick, solid 225 pounds, I was strong. I could run faster than most on the team and leap almost as high as I was tall. That ability allowed me to catch balls that were uncatchable. As a freshman, without even playing a down, I had NFL scouts already calling my name. Though football had been good to me, it hadn't always been great. A lot of pressure and troubles come with the notoriety.

So I quickly said, "Don't y'all even try to forget, I didn't practice for most of the summer due to a recurring injury. What, y'all think it's easy to watch y'all get out there and do your thing?"

"Aw, come on, Perry," Deuce said. Deuce was also African American. He was a star running back and went to high school with Lance. Out of all the freshman players, he and I were the only ones who won a place on the first string. "I had to prove myself to get on Coach Red's list. You ain't really have to do all that. He signed you up to be his main man in the outfield right off the bat. You know you have it easier than all of us."

As I sat there watching the three of their mouths yap about me being some kind of privileged citizen or something, I wondered why in the world it even bothered me what they thought. I had always been a pretty confident guy, but at that moment, it was like I could see my self-esteem being zapped away with each word they spoke.

Immediately I defended myself. "Wait a minute. Have any one of y'all three chumps had a girlfriend tried to kill herself over y'all Negroes?"

"Is that politically correct, calling me a Negro?" Collin said in his proper and uptight voice.

Mr. Cox was the other white-boy suite mate. Collin was from Alabama. He's supposed to have a great leg to kick through the uprights, but he'd been a little inconsistent during the summer practices. The coach and the rest of the team were now skeptical that he'd be able to carry us in the event our first-string kicker could not play.

Lance picked up a pillow and bopped him on the head, "Man, he just playing. We're roommates; we're brothers in a sense. Haven't we got through the whole racial thing?"

"I was just asking," Collin said, looking like a teacher had reprimanded him.

"So back to my question—have any of you had that? Don't be looking all crazy," I said to them as their mouths shut at the same time.

They all drew closer to me to hear the details. Thinking back on the scary incident, I couldn't even believe the day I found Tori, my old girlfriend of three years, sitting in her car trying to OD on the toxins. If I hadn't gotten there and opened up the car door, who knows what would have happened to her. My point, of course, wasn't to brag that I was all that and that she had to go to such lengths because she had lost me, but the dudes were saying that I was drama-free. Certainly that incident alone would get them the heck off my back.

"Whatever, man, a little girlfriend problem ain't nothing that major. My girl got pregnant!" Deuce said. "And though she gave up the baby for adoption, it's not a week that goes by that I don't think about the child I fathered."

He had me. I remembered the pregnancy scare that happened to my homeboy Cole. Another one of my boys, Damarius, got an STD. I had to be with him through that. But it wasn't me. Though I was deeply affected, I wasn't even trying to plead my case like that.

"My best friend almost killed me," Lance admitted.

"What?" I said shocked.

Deuce chimed in, "Yeah, because he tried to take his girl. Lance is not a real loyal friend. You know that firsthand, Perry, don't you?"

I chuckled. I certainly did remember when I first got to college and Lance made moves on my new girl, Savoy. In his defense, technically she was fair game. Savoy and I weren't going together any longer because right before we came to college, I had broken her trust by sleeping with my former girl, Tori, the one who tried to kill herself because I had left her.

Yeah, I had a lot of issues going on. I used to get myself in deeper, deeper, and deeper. Now that I was in college, I wanted to make sure I did things the right way. It was time for me to grow up and carry less baggage around. I knew it was going to be hard enough to make it at Georgia Tech.

"But, have you ever been hemmed up by police?" Deuce asked me. "Probably not, because you aren't the average black man. Folks don't mess with Perry Skky Jr. You're royalty in this state."

I had to tell him about a few months back. "Aw, see, I was in Hilton Head . . ."

"Well, that explains whatever bull you were about to try to feed us. You weren't even in Georgia," Deuce said, as if cops in our state were the meanest jokers around.

"Naw, y'all gonna listen," I said, knowing that I was dealt with unfairly. "I see this cute girl on the beach late one night. She's crying and all, and I'm the only one out there. I was actually trying to catch up with the other players on the team who went to this little camp. Chaplain hooked it up for us. Thought it was going to be a vacation. Shoot . . . I go to help her, turns out she had been raped, and then these three white dudes come along. Bash my face, all assuming I'm the one that messed with her. Next thing I know, the cops jack me up without any interrogation. Finally the girl comes to and tells them it wasn't me. She was date raped. What's even more a trip, the girl goes to Tech. She's a freshman here, too."

"Ooh, small world," Deuce said.

"Yeah, if she was real cute, I need to meet her," Lance teased.

Quickly I told him, "Please, you aren't her type. I saw her last week, and she wants me."

Lance, Deuce, and I laughed and kept messing with each other. We wanted to find out which one of us was the toughest. All three of us thought we had had it the roughest. However, when Collin spoke, he had us all beat.

Collin said, "Have any of you ever wanted to take your own life?"

All jokes were put aside at that point. We didn't know whether he was playing or was serious. We didn't know what in the world he was talking about. We had no idea where that comment even came from, but it certainly made us stop and be serious for a moment.

All of a sudden, Lance broke the silence and said, "Nah, I've never wanted to do that."

Deuce said, "Nah, I ain't never want to do that either."

Something inside me made me ask, "Why, Collin? You've been there?"

Collin yelled, "Just forget it." He got up from our family room area and went into his own bedroom.

When he slammed the door, instantly I prayed aloud: "Lord, my boy Collin has issues. Actually, all three of us do. You know I didn't even want to open up. In Jesus's name I pray. Amen."

When I opened my eyes, I was surprised to hear Deuce say, "You talk to the Lord often? I need to do it more."

"Yeah, partner, I understand," I responded. "We need to stick to keeping each other accountable."

Deuce and I slapped hands.

Lance cut in and said, "Enough of the mushy stuff. Let's get ready for the big party. We're headed to the big national championship game. I can feel it. We might as well celebrate early."

"You really think we got a shot?" I asked him, doubting my own abilities to help lead a team to that type of victorious season.

Confidently, Lance replied, "If I get to start, then I'll guarantee it."

I so wanted his type of buoyancy. Looking back on all I'd been through the last year had really taken a toll on my psy che. However, that was all in the past. I couldn't use my i sues as a crutch. I was a college freshman. Time for me walk positively and enjoy my life. I really hoped I could co quer my negative thinking.